FAKE DATES AND FERRY TALES

A GREENSEA ISLAND ADVENTURE

BOOK 3

JULIE FARLEY

FOG HOUSE
PRESS

"Gossip is the most powerful force in the world [and on Greensea]."
-Thomas Hardy

GREENSEA GAZETTE

Islanders,

The Big Dark is over. Frogs are croaking. Geese are honking. Sea lions are feasting on herring. The hint of spring in the air is mocking us. We know. We know. It's just a tease. We'll have our puffy vests and fuzzy boots on until July. But let us have this moment. Let us put the convertible tops down and revel in the few rays of sun. Take out the sunglasses. Roll up your sleeves. Put nail polish on the dogs and set them free. Who knows, maybe someone will sprinkle some "ferry" dust and let us enjoy a true spring.

Island PSA: The Girl Scout moms have made fifty trips to the official Cookie Cupboard, filling island minivans with cookies, and the girls are now selling the goods outside of Island Grocers. Make sure you get your Thin Mints before the food and beverage manager from Thin Pines Country Club clears them out. We all know Thin Pines would not be the same without the never-ending supply of free Thin Mints at the self-serve snack bar, but we also know we must stock our own personal pantries and freezers. Note: The Girl Scouts have moved to the Square app for cookie payment, and twenty-five percent is the strongly encouraged minimum tip amount. Yes, this tipping for barely lifting a finger trend has become excessive, but these girls have to pay for those badges somehow. Let's support our Island Scouts!

XOXO,

GG

CHAPTER ONE

"When I said I'd play doubles, I figured it would be you and me against Sylviane and Tippy," I say to my brother Josh. "Boys vs. Girls, bro!"

Josh looks at his girlfriend, Sylviane. Man, he's whipped. Can't even decide without looking to her for advice. He's the guy who hated tourists. Couldn't stand newcomers. And now, here he is, fawning over Greensea's newest resident. Love makes you do the darndest things. But he's still my brother, and blood's stronger than water last time I checked. That's why I'm here supporting him on this pickleball court.

"Happy to have you on the opposite team," says Tippy, bouncing a ball on her paddle. "Your head can be my target."

TFM. Tippy Freaking Meadowcroft. We can never be on the same team. We're worse than oil and water. We don't mix at all. Think Batman and Joker or Tom and Jerry. I pulled her hair in first grade because I wanted to see if her red curls would bounce back or if her hair would go straight, and we've been enemies ever since. We've grown slightly more civil as adults, and now she's friends with Sylviane, but we laid the ground-work for our relationship years ago and there's no fixing it at this point. Torturing Tippy is my favorite pastime. She's my go-to target and always a worthy adversary.

"Okay, you two," Sylviane chimes in. "Last I checked, this was a friendly match. Tip, you've been bugging me to play with you."

"Operative word being you! Just you!" Tippy puts on her visor as she makes her point.

The sun's out after a streak of twenty-some rainy days, and island residents are acting like they've been freed from jail. Kids are laughing as they climb on the ferry structure at the play-ground. Bike bells ding in the distance. Referee whistles rival the bird calls. The entire island's outside. Not sure how we got a court at Sunset Tower Park, but lucky us. Insert large eye roll.

Tippy and Sylviane walk over to the other side of the net. Tippy may be dressed in a fancy outfit—green skirt, matching green-and-white striped sweater, white shoes that have a green stripe on them, and tall green socks—that makes her look like she knows what she's doing, but I'm certain my baseball and natural athletic skills will parlay into excellence out here. Look out, Tippy. Someone's about to own you on the court.

"You know the rules, Dave?" Tippy asks.

I do not, in fact, know the rules, but I'm one hundred percent certain they're not that hard to figure out. I give her a thumbs up.

"It's just tennis for rich people," I add.

"Two Greensea dads who were looking to occupy their kids during summer break started pickleball in their driveway. Not rich people!" Tippy serves the ball to me.

I charge the net and whack it into the chain-link fence at the back of the court, causing people on the other court to stop and look and a dog passing by to bark. Sylviane falls down to the ground to get out of the way of my return like she was about to be hit with a flaming arrow instead of a plastic wiffle ball even though it wasn't even close and Tippy just stands there as it whizzes by her ear.

"Take it easy!" Sylviane yells as she stands back up.

"Dude, you're going to hurt someone if you hit it like that. Think ping-pong, not grand slam." Josh's out here protecting the girls.

"Sorry, guess my innate strength is just too much for the little plastic ball."

"And stay out of the kitchen!" Tippy yells.

I do. All the time. Unless it's cooking a sauce for the precious oysters I harvest, I do as little as I can in the kitchen, but I'm not sure what that has to do with the game we're playing right now.

Tippy stares at me. "I can see the little speech bubbles coming out of your head, Dave. The kitchen is the area around the net. I thought you indicated you knew how to play?"

Josh gives me a glare. There's no way he thought this was going to be a relaxing game. Nothing between Tippy and me is relaxing. We're competition central. Take that time I raced her climbing a rope in PE class. I thought my height would give me an enormous advantage, but she beat me because of her core strength. I went so fast and so hard my palm started bleeding with rope burns. I didn't stop hearing about that until sixth grade, when I took her down in wall ball at lunch. Yeah, I got in trouble for taunting and had to do lunch detention for a week. But it was worth it. I beat Tippy. In middle school, teachers kept us separated as much as possible. She had first lunch, and I had second, or vice versa. Eliminating any extra competition. It didn't make a difference. We always found a way.

Tippy serves again. Josh returns it this time with a bounce.

Nice and gentle. She sends it back my way. I have the urge to slam it again but I hit it softly.

"Out!" Tippy's made herself line umpire.

"No way, Tippy." I look to Sylviane and Josh for confirmation. Sylviane shakes her head, as does Josh.

"It was out, bro."

"Do over." I'm going to exhaust all my options before I give up a point to TFM.

"Your point." Josh looks to the girls. He has other ideas.

Sylviane serves this time. Josh hits it back.

I turn and look at Josh before they can hit it back to us. "What was that? It's like a gimme when you do it that soft!"

"It's called a dink, Dave. It's an actual strategy in pickleball." Tippy smiles like she's adding up points with her words. She hits it back and I return it with less force than before.

"Carry!" The red headed menace has a lot to say.

I drop my paddle. "I hit the ball not too hard, not too soft. What's wrong now?"

"You carried." Josh holds his paddle out. "The ball stayed with the paddle for too long."

"This is like playing pickleball with Goldilocks! How am I supposed to play?" I ask.

Tippy walks over to the bench.

"Where are you going? Too scared?" I taunt in my best fourth grade voice.

"No. You're acting like a child. I take things like this seriously and don't need you degrading what I'm doing."

I take things seriously too. Every minute I spend with my oysters is valuable for my business and the environment, so taking time out to play pickleball today is difficult when I'm trying to save the world one oyster at a time. Time is money, and eight to ten grams of carbon ions per bivalve.

Sylviane runs over to talk to Tippy. I can't hear what they're saying, but it doesn't seem to make a difference. They hug, and Tippy picks up her bag and walks off the court.

"Thanks, Syl and Josh, for trying." She waves to them.

Josh raises his paddle as a goodbye. Tippy takes the visor off and the ponytail holder out of her hair, letting it down before she grabs her helmet and scoots off on her bike.

"Nice," is all Sylviane can manage.

"Bro, you're thirty-two years old. Think it's time to act like a grown-up."

"Dude, if those are actual rules for this game, it's a little ridiculous."

Besides, I can't act my age. I don't know how when Tippy's around. Some chemical in my brain causes me to behave like a toddler who's lost his favorite toy. Maybe it's just a habit after all these years. You know what they say, old habits die hard. Or maybe it's a Pavlovian response. Regardless, I don't know how to stop doing it. When Tippy Meadowcroft's around, I act like a buffoon, not the guy who was just interviewed on NPR to discuss the benefits of oyster farming to our local ecosystem. I'm not the guy who would move a spider instead of smashing it with the bottom of my shoe or the guy who let the family of deer clear-cut his hydrangeas.

The gate to the court closes behind us as we walk to our cars. Sylviane and Josh hop into her beloved Honda Pilot she named Old Blue. As I head to my truck, I see a box turtle lumbering out into the parking lot straight toward Old Blue. I yell, "Stop!" but they don't hear me. I run to the back of the car, hit the window with my palm, and bend down to save the precious creature, just as Old Blue lurches to a stop.

"What the hell, Dave?" yells Josh as he jumps out of the car.

"Oh my gosh! Are you okay?" asks Sylviane. She sees me mid-bend.

"Had to save this little fellow." I hold up the turtle, who's pulled his head and all of his arms and legs into his shell.

"I thought I hit you!" Sylviane's eyes bug out of her head.

"Dude, you scared the crap out of us and almost got run over, all for a turtle."

"Yep." I did, because it's a harmless little creature who was about to be squashed by a multi-ton vehicle. Duh.

"You couldn't have shown an ounce of the compassion you have for that turtle when we were playing pickleball?" Josh asks.

"What do you mean?"

"You almost took Tippy's head off with the ball and argued about whether or not your shot was in or out." Josh stands with his hands on his hips, just like Dad.

"That's because she's Tippy, and we always do that. And this is a tiny animal who was in distress. You know I can't stand seeing anything get hurt."

I'd do almost anything to ensure that no living creature is hurt or upset. Except, I guess, play like a reasonable person if Tippy is involved.

CHAPTER TWO

DAVE

I reach down, pull the wet, succulent creature to my mouth, and give her a little kiss. I'm addicted to the hard exterior shell and the opalescent, moist, luscious jewel that lies beneath the surface. Touching them, holding them, feeling them in my fingers—it's my happy place.

I'm the calmest when my feet are six inches deep in the mucky bay, sea water rocking up against my waders, talking to my bivalves. Piles of oysters clustered on top of each other, waiting for me to harvest them. Their shells look spiny and ugly to most, but to me they're perfection and just the right size to hold in my palm. My fingers wrap around the shell just tight enough to feel its heft, placing each one in the bucket before I bring them home.

My second favorite part of the oyster experience is shucking them. Using my grandpa's knife to pry open their shell. Looking at the pearly, creamy center. Each one better than the last. And forget it, when one slides down my throat...heaven.

My brothers say I'm married to my shells. I don't disagree.

Well, I'd at least call them by their proper name—bivalves. They're filled with a pleasure second to none. They don't tell me what to do, and they let me act like an obsessive fan. To top it off, everyone loves them and clambers for them—well, at least the people I want to spend time with do.

And have I mentioned they're saving the shoreline, hence the world? Each magnificent shell cleaning the water we all love. Stopping coastal erosion. Creating homes for other marine life. And to top it off, they make pearls. Never has there been a more perfect creature. The jewel of the sea and a diamond in my life.

I harvest all my oysters in Bungalow Bay, or Bungy Bay if you're a local, right across the street from my house. The protected cove coupled with an active tide swing makes it a perfect bay to swim in and to raise oysters. I live and work within a twenty-yard span. I have a little oyster shack, about the size of a couple of telephone booths, in the little grassy cove between the street and the water's edge.

I carry today's harvest up to the shack and flip the sign to open. They'll sell out in an hour. Always do. I used to carry buckets of oysters around town to sell to the restaurants, but since I built this thing, people come to me. No more Delivery Dave, and I prefer it this way. More time with my creatures and saving the earth.

The chef from The Claw, Hunter Sorenson, is always my first customer, and my most discerning. I want to be annoyed with the time he takes to select which oysters he's going to purchase, but I respect it. He, like me, appreciates the value of each one.

"Hey, Hunt! Usual?"

He buys four dozen a day. In emergency situations, when he sells out, I'll still run some down to the restaurant midday. He serves them raw, like they're meant to be, sometimes with a

Japanese or a French dressing or some kind of chutney. Always changing it up by the season.

"You know it," he says, pulling out a wad of cash. "Best-selling item on my menu, D."

"Sure it's not just because of the Sherman name on the menu? Close proximity to Johnny Nickel?"

Ever since my sister, Jac, started dating that rockstar, visitors to the island have increased along with collectible souvenirs. There are Johnny Nickel mugs, stickers, and t-shirts sold at all the tourist shops. Johnny licensed some one-of-a-kind designs to the island to help generate a little extra cash for the stores. The town meeting, with all the store owners deciding who would sell what item, was bananas, but Mayor Nickerbottom settled on a rotation of goods every three months in case one item gained in popularity and another died out. The mayor made sure that no business owner would be left behind. In return for Johnny's generosity, islanders are pretty good about keeping his where-abouts a secret. He's built a mutual respect between the locals and his privacy. But I'd be lying if I said I didn't second guess people's motives from time to time.

"I don't get many Johnny Nickel fans at The Claw."

"True, too high brow and expensive for his fourteen-year-old fangirls."

The Claw is Greensea's only James Beard-nominated restaurant, as Hunter likes to remind people. I'm sure he's hoping the Michelin gang will hop on the ferry and make their way over to him. And you know what? Kudos if they do, because this guy works harder than most. If he spends a tenth of the time he takes picking out oysters on the rest of the stuff, it's impressive. He's about as all-in as you can get.

"Own it, man. You have the best oysters out there."

I can't help but smile. I'm a proud dad on graduation day. These oysters are my crowning glory.

"I know you're out there every day talking to them, and it shows."

I put my hands together and bow my head in thanks. He gets me.

Hunter gives me a salute and jumps back in his old Chevy Blazer with his golden retriever, Rags, sitting in the backseat.

"See ya, Hunt."

Topper Meadowcroft pulls up in his meticulously kept white Chrysler Sebring convertible next. You'd think it was brand new and not two decades old because of the way it shines. If you pull into a parking spot near him, you're liable to find him buffing his hood with a cotton cloth or using his tiny vac to remove some pine needles from the seats. Today he's dressed to the nines: white hair covered by a straw hat, light blue plaid button-down shirt, and pressed chinos—the dress pant type, not the ones you get at The Gap.

"Morning, Dave!"

Topper's most famous accessory is his smile. If his teeth could twinkle, they would. It's not a cursory smile he throws around, it's warm and from his heart.

"Hey, Topper. What can I do you for?"

I'm a tad worried he may be coming to complain about my aggression on the pickleball court with his daughter.

"Well, you know I'm not here to get any of this sea life."

Topper, or his daughter, Tippy, would no sooner be shucking oysters than they would be wading in the mucky bay. Topper may be the most gentile islander I've ever met, and within that description, he does not touch my slimy critters. Instead, he runs *The Greensea Gazette*. As far as I can tell, he is the sports, food, and news writer. The only thing he doesn't do, I guess, is write the damn gossip column.

"I have a favor to ask. We need some lights at the pickleball court," says Topper. "Tippy has an idea to offer lessons and date nights on the court, but we need some lights out under the shelter. Think you could stop by Meadowcroft to look and see if it would work?"

Meadowcroft...You never know if they're referring to themselves or their property, Meadowcroft Acres, which might as well be a character in all our lives. Eight pristine acres up near the forest. Flower farm and stand. The main house belongs to Topper and his wife, Bell. Another house on the far side of the property near the court belongs to Tippy, their beloved daughter. And now, they've covered the pickleball court so it can be used all year round. While Topper stays busy with the newspaper, Bell owns Bell's (do you see a theme with naming things after themselves?), a store that specializes in tablescapes. They sell tablecloths, placemats, and centerpieces. Hard for me to believe that's even a thing.

"Have electricity out there?"

"Sure do, but it's just a plug."

"I should be able to work with that. I'll come out in the next couple of days and take a look." My side hustle as a handyman helps to fund my passion project.

"Thanks, Dave. Tip will be thrilled."

Tippy may be thrilled to have lights, but I'm certain she wouldn't have called me since we're not BFFs. Especially after the debacle on the court.

"Does she know I'm doing it?"

"No, and no need to tell her. She's always out and about anyway. Probably won't ever know how it got done. The important thing is getting it done, and you're the best guy for the job."

Topper tips his hat and gets into his car. I suppose I can take care of that for Topper, not his daughter.

GREENSEA GAZETTE

Scenes from everyone's favorite pickleball court brought us visions of the eldest Sherman brother trying to off his rival with the long red hair using a neon-yellow pickleball. Have no fear, she kept herself safe by storming off on her broom—I mean bike.

The founders of the courts have raised enough money for the large iron gate at the front of the courts, memorializing their legacy. There will be a plaque with the official Governor-approved story so that no other island is keen to steal Greensea's legacy once again. Shall we remind you of the grand history of the sport?

Paul Prenderson, longtime resident of Pickles Harbor, loved playing tennis with his kids, but didn't have enough room in his driveway to make a full tennis court, so he invented a paddle game called pickleball. His devious cousin, Phil Prenderson, resident of another PNW island, came for a visit and enjoyed playing the game so much he brought it home with him. Thus began the decades-long war of the origin of pickleball. Thankfully, our own Gazette had pictures of Paul and family playing the game in their driveway that outdated anything his cousin Phil could find. That, coupled with the fact that Phil also stole Paul's famous lasagna recipe, was enough to prove that Paul was the creator and Phil was just the liar. I mean, duh, we have Pickles Harbor. Of course it originated here!

Island wars are real. So are wars within families. Maybe even more real than Tippy Meadowcroft and Dave Sherman fighting on the court.

XOXO,

GG

CHAPTER THREE

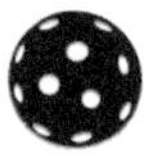

Taking old (not in the literal age definition of the word) Bertha out for a spin down to Pilates class is my favorite way to start my day. The damp spring breeze blows through my hair, giving it an extra curl, as I let it flow behind me like a flag on my morning bike ride.

Riding around on Bertha gives me a chance to see what's going on around Greensea, allowing me to gather notes for the gossip column I inherited after Don Hamilton died. My dad didn't know who else to ask without blowing Don's cover. I was the easy (and only) answer. I know how the paper works because I've been working there as an admin, a bookkeeper, an occasional photographer, and a sometimes editor. You name it, I do it. I'm Dad's right hand.

Lucky for me, no one suspects a bike rider to be gathering information for GG. It's the perfect cover. I mean, how can I take notes on all the happenings when I'm on a bike? Wink. Wink. What no one realizes is that I have a photographic memory. It's the only way I got through AP Bio all those years ago. Everything I see when I'm out and about gets etched into my brain. I know how many coffees Jeannie Templeton brings to work at Island Realty each day—three. She used to bring four, but she's convinced Nora Cunningham is getting to each house Jeannie is scheduled to show and burning something in the oven before Jeannie and her clients arrive. So, no coffee for Nora.

Timing my bike rides with ferry departures gives me a full picture of many islanders' routines. Dad told me Don used to hang out at coffee shops, but sitting in one place for extended periods of time is not my style. So, I put the pedals to the metal.

Dayton Riverside usually takes the 7:05 ferry, but something's got a bee in his bonnet and he's getting on the 6:20 now. He's also given himself a glow up. All shined up, looking spiffy as he heads into the office. There's not one hair out of place on his head. Trying to impress someone, but I've yet to figure out whom.

My morning ride doesn't allow me to observe everyone's routine, of course; those work-from-home people are elusive. But I stick to the mainstays of the island and get to see enough to write a column every day.

I lock Bertha up in front of The Reformation, the old church-turned-Pilates studio, and head into class, another key place to find fodder for my column. The Reformation has twelve reformers—exercise equipment resembling medieval torture devices—lined up and waiting for the lucky class participants. Most of us are regulars, meeting day after day at nine AM.

Walking into the sanctuary, I notice someone on my reformer. Laura Prescott's bold enough to occupy my machine today. How dare she? We all use the same machines every day, with few exceptions. I like the way the light shines through the old stained glass windows in my particular spot. It's in front of a mirror but not too close to the dreaded altar that gives me the creeps. Close enough to the bathroom if I need it (which I never do, but better safe than sorry) and close enough to the holy-water-font-turned-water-cooler. And my spot centers me within the sanctuary—ready to glean any tidbits that may or may not make their way into GG's next column.

"Eh hem." I clear my throat at the end of the reformer.

"Oh, hi, Tippy! How are you?" Laura looks up from adjusting her straps.

"I'd be better if you weren't on my machine."

"Your reformer? So sorry. I didn't know we reserved certain ones."

Umm. Not true. She's usually on the machine closest to the altar. Laura goes to get up, and a moment of guilt rushes over me. "It's fine. Sorry. I shouldn't have insinuated that. I'll take this one."

Breathe in. Breathe out. The one right next to her is free. More glare from the red stained glass window, but I'll survive.

I'm trying to relax, to not be so wound up about every little thing. Even a minor detour in my routine knocks me for a loop. City crews were trimming branches around the power lines last week, and it set me back three minutes on my ride, making me miss the regulars on their morning jaunts. I jumped off my bike, got the name of the crew manager, and was about to shoot off a harshly worded email to the powers-that-be about the inefficiencies in their system, but I took a deep breath and thought better of it. Podcasts have helped me learn to meditate and breathe through these minor issues, but it's a learning process and not my natural inclination. Most of the time, Pilates helps me find my Zen, but it doesn't when someone steals my reformer.

Regardless, it is a great place to get the scoop on what's happening on the island. Like last week, everyone had their leggings in a knot over the kale that was substituted for arugula in the Greens on the Green salad at Thin Pines Country Club. Martha, our instructor, would kick me out if she knew I collected information from my classmates like some people collect seashells.

"Welcome to the church of Pilates. Get ready to pray at our altar." Martha's irreverent start to every class cueing me to take a deep breath.

"Heels in parallel on the foot bar, open with an exhale. Keep your back in neutral. Connect those front ribs, Tippy. And inhale on the return. Ten more."

Connect my front ribs? How did I disconnect them? No matter how many classes I take, there's still room for improvement and further understanding (or confusion).

"And two, one. Reach back and grab your straps and put them on your feet."

I never get used to lying on my back with my legs extended out in front of me in straps. My favorite seventy-year-old, Cheryl, giggles like a preteen boy, which has a domino effect and we all snicker.

Martha ignores us and tells us to move our legs in circles.

"Sit up, using your core, and stand facing the poles."

"Ow!" yells Laura. I peek over. She's still lying down and grabbing at her head.

"What's wrong?" Martha asks, rushing to her reformer.

"My hair's stuck!"

Martha bends down and gives Laura's blonde locks a good pull. She takes out her phone from the pocket in her workout tights and shines the flashlight on the nest of hair. She tugs a little more, and Laura pushes her hand away.

"That hurts!" Laura scolds.

"Well, girl, I think we need to extricate the hair with some scissors."

Laura looks at Martha, sighs, and says, "Do what you need to do. I can't stay like this."

I whisper "karma" under my breath and give a little laugh.

"Really, Tip? If I didn't know better, I'd think you rigged this machine to make this happen," says Laura. My whisper is never as soft as I think it is.

Martha stands up and moves toward the reception desk near the baptismal font. "The rest of you put your feet in the shoulder rests, hands on the foot bar, and plank."

She comes back with a Swiss Army knife and pulls out the scissor tool, ready to free Laura. I giggle every time I glimpse the procedure going on next to me and almost choke on my gum. I try to swallow it before Martha notices, but it won't go down.

Martha cuts off some of Laura's hair, then stands up and points at me. "You know the rules. No gum! It's for your own safety. I've never done the Heimlich maneuver on a real person."

I hate that rule. Gum makes me calm. It's a meditation in my mouth. And sometimes it stops me from saying something stupid because I chew it for a minute before I speak. Laura should be happy I have gum, and I'm not making comments about her new 'do.

"Push back with your arms. Come home with your hips up." Martha's the queen of directing us, even when she has to multitask. Somehow, I survive the rest of class and even find a few moments of Zen.

Cheryl walks up to me as I'm wiping down the reformer. "Sweetie, I want to set you up with my nephew, Darren."

I finish wiping down the foot bar and stand up. Darren's a couple of years older than me, but the only memory I have of him is when Mom and Dad took me to a Greensea High football game and he streaked across the field. I've already seen it all. No need to revisit.

I give her a quick hug. "You know I'm ready to cast my net a bit wider than Greensea, Cheryl. But thank you."

"Well, you've got to do more than spar with Dave Sherman on the pickleball court if you want to find love."

Ouch. Score one for Cheryl.

I love my Pilates crew. We have this unspoken bond as we lie on the reformers together day after day. Ranging in age from twenty-five to seventy, the only thing in common is the terror we get from flamingo and legs in straps. Oh, but of course, we have a common history. We're all islanders and some of us have known each other for most of our lives. But I still don't want them to set me up. Tippy Meadowcroft is the only one in charge of her love life.

"Iconic, Laura," says Farrah on the way out. She rumples Laura's hair. "Shag cuts are all the rage now!"

The bike ride home's uneventful other than Amanda Willow speeding down Miller in her minivan with a kid throwing a Pop-Tart out the window. Late for school again, Willows! What is going on in that house?

At least the morning outing gave me enough info for the column. Mission accomplished.

It's only a seven-minute ride to my house. Today I make it in six and a half, and Bear, my toy poodle and currently the only true love of my life, greets me at my door. I put him under my arm and sit at my laptop to prep a little more for my Monday morning video meeting, because there's no such thing as being too prepared.

GREENSEA GAZETTE

Dear Islanders,

Well, well, well. The St. Paddy's Day Festival at the waterfront was great. Great until the little rascal turned the sprinklers on the Irish dancers. Fingers have been pointed and excuses have been made. But we can't help but wonder if the white shirts the dancers were wearing prompted the teenagers to start their own wet t-shirt contest.

The bash at the O'Donnells' home went a little overboard per usual. Keg stands aren't a good look for the over-fifty crowd. Take that back, for the over-twenty-two crowd.

Greensea Naturals has its Shamrock kombucha on sale this week. It may have been a bit over fermented, as there are reports of many empty cans being found at Gulls Point after a few late-night parties. Please remember to recycle and clean up after yourselves, Islanders!

And make sure to check out Laura Prescott's new haircut! It is not, as she might have you believe, because of an encounter with a permanent green dye.

XOXO,

GG

CHAPTER FOUR

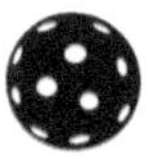

TIPPY

"Tippy, your submission for *Love at the Last Resort* blew us away. Greensea pops on the page. We can only imagine it will be even better on screen."

"Thank you!" That was my goal. I spent days coming up with reasons our little island would be a perfect destination for everyone's favorite dating survival show. What a personal coup this would be. Jac Sherman's responsible for Greensea hitting the Top 40 with Johnny Nickel's hit "Greensea Gal." But getting Greensea on Netflix's top ten...that could be all my doing.

"Let me just do a couple of quick introductions of our *Love at the Last Resort* team. I'm Andrew Collins, and we also have Melinda Sanchez and Charles Cohen here today." Andrew straightens the collar of his blue-and-white striped shirt, and the camera pans out to the entire group on the Zoom call. It's like they have a professional cameraman instead of a little camera on top of their laptops.

"Before we dig into our Greensea questions, I always like to understand a little more about the person I'm meeting with and their motivations for doing something. Why don't you begin by telling us a little more about you and your desire to bring *Love at the Last Resort* to your lovely hometown?" Andrew gives me a made-for-TV smile.

These people get right down to business. I feel like I'm on an exclusive interview with Oprah, not just your average run-of-the-mill video call. The question's not what I was expecting, but I'm quick on my feet.

"Well, everyone always asks how I got the name Tippy, and I'm sure you're wondering too. My dad's name is Topper. When I was little, I always wanted to be with him. I'd hang out under his desk while he wrote stories for our local paper. Follow him around everywhere on our family farm, hoping for a ride on his shoulders." A little "ah" comes across the laptop. "In addition to that, I also had a penchant for climbing. Fences. Check. Tables. Check. Backs of sofas. Check. Bookcases. Check. Dressers. Check. Check. My parents spent copious amounts of time securing things to walls when I was a toddler. I even climbed the Christmas tree one year with little success."

"Sounds like you were a handful!" says Andrew.

"Yes. I guess my parents would agree. So one of my first words was 'tippy,' as in 'tippy top.' I wanted to be at the tippy top of everything, whether it was furniture or my dad's shoulders. I always wanted to be on the tippy top of Topper. Hence my nickname."

Living on a small island meant things like nicknames made their way through the trails and over the bays quickly. Reminding the teachers that I still wanted to be Tippy and not Lisbeth (why my parents chose this, I don't know) on the first day of school was annoying, but it was a small price to pay for my one-of-a-kind name.

My parents weren't game to change my name for me

legally, so I did it as soon as I graduated from high school and turned eighteen. No one could stop me then. So now, my driver's license, passport, and deed for my house all say Tippy Meadowcroft. And I couldn't be happier.

I guess my name became my mantra. The word that pulses through my blood. The first thing I say when I wake up in the morning. My guiding principle. I want to be the tippy top of everything I can be. And nothing is going to stop me, even on this call.

"Love a good backstory," says Andrew. "Now, what motivated you to apply for this?"

I have my elevator pitch all set.

"Well, as you know, Greensea's own Jac Sherman had a role in the first season of *Love at Last Resort*, and then Greensea became a household name with Johnny Nickel's hit song. It's the perfect time to capitalize on all of that and to put Greensea on the map for the amazing location it is."

"True, true."

I keep my other motivations for bringing the show to Greensea close to my chest.

They all nod to each other.

"Let's talk a few more specifics about Greensea," says Melinda, the woman with cat-eyeglasses and a perfect black bob. "Is there anywhere large enough for the contestants to be housed together?"

Jackpot. All set for that question.

"Of course! Greensea is home to an 8,000 square foot house used by General Swifterson during World War I. The US government built it during the Pig War, when they thought this part of the country would play a more active role in world peace. The government was looking for a secluded location, and Greensea Island fit the bill. They built the home to look like a regal estate so, if discovered, no one would guess it could house troops if necessary. Now the grounds are home to an arboretum with dozens of walking trails. The house is only open during the holidays, but I know we could rent it for the show."

"Interesting. A bit of a history," mentions Charles, who nods his head of salt-and-pepper hair.

"It's historic, but it has all the amenities like heat, air conditioning, and, of course, indoor plumbing." Laughs all around. Scored another point. No need to mention there aren't enough beds in the house and the other furnishings are quite slim. Should we need to, I'm sure Greensea residents will step up and provide everything the house needs. And the network must come in with certain basic items like linens and all of that.

"Great. Great," says Andrew. "You've told us about some of the scenic spots. The bluffs at Gulls Point. Paddling in Bungalow Bay. Sunrise over the Cascades and sunset over the Olympics. There won't be any shortage of scenic vantage points."

"And don't forget the ferry," I add. "The only way on and off Greensea is via boat, which allows for a great deal of secrecy and adventure."

The island's magic lives with the ferry. Tell anyone you live on an island only accessible by boat, and they get starry-eyed. It's filled with wonder and enchantment, but it's not the most convenient way of life. For instance, when I played field hockey in high school, we missed the late ferry one night coming back from a game and had to wait until four in the morning to get home. Picture twenty teenaged girls stuck on a school bus together for five hours overnight. Not pretty. Very petty. But I'll keep the underbelly of ferry life to myself for this call and focus on the magic.

"Yes. Yes. All of that sounds ideal," says Charles.

Melinda scoots her glasses up on her nose and pipes up. "So, you've told us a great deal about the location, but what about the people on Greensea? Will they be well suited for our show? What does a potential bachelor pool look like?"

Shit. I'd assumed (and hoped) they'd bring (intriguing) people, and we'd just be the location. I didn't think the residents of Greensea would be the subjects of the show. Imagine Dave Sherman or one of those guys as the bachelors? He'd be carrying a bucket of sea slop and Greensea would end up the laughing-stock of America.

"Ms. Meadowcroft, did you hear the question?" asks Andrew.

"Yes. Sorry. Trying to think of the best way to sum up the people here." As the writer of the notorious GG, I should be able to do that pretty well. But all I can think of are everyone's shortcomings and not how to sell them. "Greensea has plenty of bachelors and bachelorettes who will be colorful on camera."

I jump when I hear a drill outside the window. Two of the people cover their ears. What the hell is going on? I turn around to look. Flipping Dave Sherman's climbing down a ladder on the pickleball court. Like I summoned him with my thoughts! I turn around as he makes his way closer to the house.

"Ohh! Could he be one of the contestants?" asks Melinda.

I'm sitting in front of the window, meaning they can see everything that's going on behind me better than I can. Dave—floppy haired, tall, and clad in a flannel, well-worn jeans, and work boots—is behind me. Sure, his jeans outline his butt, but is there anyone who wants to see Dave's butt?

"Dave? No. No. He would never be a part of the show."

Why would they want Dave? He's an oyster farmer, not the flashy specimen they need on the show. Does he even have a six-pack, other than the one in the cooler on his front porch?

"Why not?" asks Melinda.

"Not his style," is all I can say.

"Of course, we'll want you to be our star contestant," says Andrew, who must be the head honcho.

Me? There's no way. I'm not doing this. I could be the host or a producer, add some local color. But no way, no how will I be a contestant. Tippy Meadowcroft does not willingly put herself into situations she can't control. And contestants have no control over anything.

I giggle, since every single word has now escaped me.

"Well, Tippy? As far as I can see, someone who's this excited to bring the show to their hometown should be a part of it. Unless, of course, you're already attached?" Melinda points out.

My eyes get wide. I clench and unclench my fists. I'm single. Eternally single, I'm told, because of my high standards.

"Oh my gosh. He's so cute," says Melinda. I look at my screen and see Dave standing at the window behind me like he's trying to get my attention. I turn around and give him my death stare. He purses his lips and waves.

"Is he your boyfriend, Tippy? You two make an adorable couple." She looks over at her salt-and-pepper-haired colleague. "They'd be perfect as our hosts if we choose Greensea."

I'm stunned into silence. I don't even answer. I'm not sure what to say. Shit. Dave comes up to the window again and draws a heart on it. What the hell is he doing?

"Oh my gosh! I'm so sorry! He's just the hired help!"

"Judging from the way he looked at you, there's more than hired help going on between you two," laughs Melinda.

"It's just Dave. We go way back."

"We can tell." Andrew is scribbling on a notepad.

Dave's moving his finger in a "come hither" movement as he sashays back from the window. Does he not see I'm on a video call? And what's he doing anyway? Why is he even here?

"We'll let you two get to whatever he has in mind, but we'd

like to see more of Greensea. Maybe you and your boyfriend—what was his name? Dean? Dave?—can send us a video of one of your dates in the next week. And then take one of our producers to some of your favorite spots. Let us see what it would be like for contestants on Greensea."

"Oh. Um. Well." Where are my words? What am I doing? Breathe. In. Out.

"Your chemistry is unmistakable, and he's got you tongue-tied. Love it!" Mr. Salt-and-Pepper Hair gives a laugh.

Chemistry? More like he's the baking soda you pour into the volcano of my heart. He makes me explode every time. But whatever this is, whatever they saw, they liked. Damn. Think quick. How can I fix this?

I turn around and give Dave a sultry look. Two can play this game. "There's plenty more where that came from."

"We'll be in touch. Expect a producer there in the next week, after we review your video."

I leave the meeting. Holy cow. Shit is not an adequate swear word. Let me repeat, they think Dave Sherman is my boyfriend. Call out the National Guard. Pigs must be flying and hell must've frozen over.

I put my head down on my desk. There's a lot to do. I have to send in the best video possible, and then I have to whip this island into shape before they even get here. And that can't start until I tell Dave about the mess he just created. He'll rue the day he made little gestures in my window. I get up from my chair and run out to the pickleball court. Bear follows at my heels.

CHAPTER FIVE

DAVE

Putting lights on the court is going to be a cinch. Bonus, the teasing I got in. At least I was sweeter than I was the other day on the court.

A door slams. A dog yips. And I see a flash of red hair coming toward me. Uh oh. Someone doesn't feel the same way about my harmless little prank.

"What the hell was that, Dave?" Tippy yells as she speed walks across the grass and onto the pickleball court.

"Just playing, Tip. Just playing. Trying to make up for all my antics on the court the other day." See, I was being nice, not acting like I wanted to take her out.

"What are you even doing here?"

"Topper asked me to set up some lights for you. Sounds like you have some harebrained idea about pickleball lessons at night?"

"It's not harebrained. It's all part of my larger plan." She's huffing and puffing like she's just run a marathon.

I give her a good once-over from the top of the ladder.

"A larger plan? Total Greensea domination?" I crack myself up. "Just having some fun, Tip." I take another look at her. "What're you wearing?"

She looks down. An emerald green silk shirt with a bow tied around her neck and flamingo-printed pajama pants. She's business on top and sleep on the bottom.

"I was on a video work call!"

"On video? Can't you take care of all of your business at Saltwater Bakeshop?" Video calls are a big city thing, not a Greensea thing.

"No! It was a meeting with some Hollywood producers."

I climb down from the ladder and examine the bottom of the wall. "Hollywood producers? What the hell are you up to now?"

"I am trying to bring the biggest reality dating show to Greensea."

I stop and look at her. She can't be. No. Has to be something different. There's no way anyone in their right mind would bring that piece of trash to our island.

"Tell me it's not what I think it is."

Tippy pulls up her pajama pants and messes with the bow around her neck.

"It's *Love at the Last Resort,* but why should you care?"

"Why should I care? Do you have amnesia? Traumatic brain injury? Did you forget the humiliation that show caused my family?"

I pack up my tools. No way I'm helping this evil person anymore.

"Of course not. But this is the redemption arc. The time to make everything right. To show Greensea differently. Not through that clown Nick's eyes."

Jac's ex-husband left her to go on that joke of a show. He wrote her a letter, stole all their savings for cosmetic surgeries, and took off. Then he had the nerve to humiliate her on TV and act like it was her fault he left. *Love at the Last Resort* will be here over my dead body.

"Well, because of your little show in front of the camera, you may have just ruined everything."

Perfect. Best thing that's come from teasing Tippy.

"Great. Then we can wash our hands of that show once and for all."

"Au contraire, Dave. Now they think you're my boyfriend. They'll be here in about a week to meet us in person."

The flashlight I'm attempting to put away drops to the ground.

"Boyfriend?" is all I can mutter.

"Yes! You were dancing around outside the window making kissy faces. What else did you expect?"

An eye roll and a middle finger was what I was going for.

"And now we have to make a video of a date, and then they're coming to Greensea to meet us and go on a day filled with romantic outings with them!" She spits it out so fast that she needs to sit down to catch her breath, only there isn't anywhere to sit, so she plops on the court and puts her head on her knees.

I take a deep breath in, one-two-three-four, and out, five-six-seven-eight. "Back up a little bit. What do these Hollywood fools think?"

"That we're dating." Tippy sighs.

I throw the last thing in my toolbox.

"Why would you tell them something stupid like that?"

"I didn't."

She's making no sense. Zero.

"They saw you making all your bedroom gestures in front of the window and thought we were together."

My left eyebrow twitches. The Tippy reaction is taking over my body, face first.

"Give me a break, Tip. I've been teasing you since we were six years old. You know it was nothing more than that."

"You're right. I do! But the three people sitting on my video meeting thought our chemistry was off the charts." Her hands are moving faster than her words.

"Who cares what some random people from the stupidest TV show in the world think? Just tell them they were wrong."

"I can't do that. This is too big." She stands up, grabs one of the pickleball paddles, and starts slamming balls from the bucket across the net.

"You're going to hurt someone if you're not careful."

"You're the only someone out here." She aims one at my head and moves it at the last minute.

I pick up another paddle and swing it like a baseball bat. "Why would you want any part of that junky show?"

Hitting the ball takes away an ounce of my anger.

She puts a hand on her hip, then says, "I thought it would be a great way to showcase Greensea and bring more tourism dollars to the island."

"Interesting. I can think of about a hundred better, and easier, ways to bring money to Greensea." I toss another ball in the air, swing at it, and miss. Now would be a good time to leave. Like drop the paddle and go. But I'm stuck in cement and left listening to this babble. My brain's sending misfires like it always does when Tippy Freaking Meadowcroft is in front of me. The air sucks all the rational sense out of me.

"Strike one." She rolls her eyes. "Anyway, they were just asking me if I was in a relationship when you drew that ridiculous heart on the window."

"Still don't get why you had to say yes."

She takes her hair out of her claw clip and runs her fingers through it. "I didn't. But one thing led to another, and now they're coming here, and you have to pretend to be my boyfriend."

I shake my head. "No way am I fake dating you, Tippy. I value my sanity and dignity way too much for that."

"Your dignity, Dave? I haven't served time. Never harmed an animal. I teach senior exercise classes for the Fit Greenies. I'm a catch!" She turns around so I can't see her face.

"Forget about the dating crap. Why would I, Dave Sherman, have anything to do with that show?"

She turns back toward me and I swear she wipes away a tear. Ignore. Don't look at her eyes. Heart, stop. Don't feel bad. Remember. It's TFM, not the box turtle Sylviane almost ran over.

"Because it will be the ultimate middle finger to Nick. He went on the show to make something of his life and couldn't. We'll show him he was the problem, not the show. He tried to blame Jac for all his failings, and that didn't work. You know they'll mention him, and we can just embarrass him a little more."

See? Regular Tippy. Any hint of tears is gone like the sunshine in December.

"Topper should have had me look at your head. You've got a screw loose."

She hits a ball across the court again.

"Please!" She throws her arms down at her side. "It will just be for one little video, and then one day when the producer is on Greensea. It will be less than twelve hours of your time. Help me. Just let me seal this deal, and then you can go on your merry way."

"I don't want to 'seal this deal.'" I use air quotes, and then the words leave my mouth before I can think better of them. "What's in it for me?"

She looks around. The engine's going in her brain. Another wicked plan. I feel it coming.

"I see your diabolical brain coming up with an evil plan to force me into submission. I'm not scared of you. So give me one good reason to do it."

Half of my brain is screaming at me for considering this, and the other half is egging me on. Angel on my right. Devil on my left.

She puts her finger to her mouth. "I'll make it a condition that they clear Jac's name in the first show! We'll let your family store be in a scene. Drive up business."

Cedar & Fern doesn't need any more business. Especially from reality TV.

"The point is, the Shermans want nothing to do with that show. Good, bad, or otherwise."

"Okay. Name it then. How much am I going to pay to get you to fake date me for one day?"

I fold up my ladder, grab my toolbox, and throw it all in the back of the truck.

"No deal, Tip."

And I drive away, not looking back so that, in case there are tears, I can't see them.

CHAPTER SIX

DAVE

Lesson learned. Never tease or try to torture Tippy Meadowcroft again. Ever. I take that back. Never ever step foot on Meadowcroft again. Never speak to Tippy again. Or her dad. Or her mother. Pretend they don't exist.

When I used to torment Tippy in school, my mom always had the same refrain: "You'll be sorry."

Well guess freaking what? I'm sorry. But the thing is, I've been doing it for so long that I don't know how not to do it. We're like magnetic bumper cars drawn to each other, but we crash and burn when we're together. Tippy knows what she wants, and nothing stands in her way. That's part of the reason it's so fun to annoy her.

I'm not paying attention as I drive and realize too late I'm speeding down the road. Before I know it, I hear the siren behind me. I pull over onto the shoulder, and Bob walks up to the window.

It takes me a second to crank the window down. "Cut me a break, Bobby. I just had an interaction with Tippy."

"If I cut everyone a break who used Tippy Meadowcroft as a reason for their dangerous driving, we wouldn't have any money to build a new police station. You were going 23.7, Dave—6.2 MPH above the speed limit. You know I can't let that go."

Bob has a mini spiral notebook out like he's one of the Hardy Boys looking for clues.

"Whatever. Just make it fast."

I pull out my license and insurance card, and Bob takes it back to his patrol car. Greensea has to be the only city in America that has a speed limit that involves a decimal point. Idiotic city council thought it was a good idea, but it has to cause more trouble than it's worth. Maybe I'll take it to the courts. Talk about distracted driving, trying to figure out where your odometer line is in between the numbers. Someone's going to run off the road trying to stay under the all-too-slow speed limit.

Bob saunters to the car and hands me the ticket.

"Slow down, son."

"Got it. I'll be under the speed limit from here on out."

"Not too slow. I can get you for that too."

I shake my head and crank the window back up. This ticket is going right to Meadowcroft as a bill. Thanks a lot, Tippy! Nothing good comes from being involved with her. Topper can find someone else to put lights up at the pickleball court. I have all the same feelings I did when we were playing Senior Assassin, and I hid in the bushes at Meadowcroft, decked out in a ghillie suit, waiting to get Tippy with my water gun. Only to have her escape out a side entrance, find the person who had my name, and get them to come tag me with the water gun while I gathered slugs. Tippy always wins, but this time I won't let her.

I need the water. The calming tide in Bungalow Bay. Harvesting some oysters will take my mind off my morning.

Everyone thought I was crazy when I bought this place right after college. It was a dump. Total fixer upper. But with a little elbow grease, I've turned it into a one-bedroom stunner. Well, a stunner for a bachelor. Complete with solar panels on the roof and a couple of rain barrels to water my small lawn. My mom and her first-class decorating style would definitely not call it fit for most. But it feels like home. I can sit on my porch and watch the tide come in and out. Make sure no one's messing with my oysters. It's peaceful and contained. Just the way I like things.

I grab my waders; today seems like a good day for red. Mom's always trying her hardest to find me waders in different colors. One year she even found a pair with smiley faces all over them.

I clomp out toward the bay—thirty-two steps from my front porch to the water's edge—and find my peace and serenity while I look at my oyster bags. I've been farming oysters for the last ten years. Started from a pile of spat and a single bag. A professor in college got me hooked on the environmental benefits of oyster farming. That, coupled with my parents always pushing me to follow my passions, led to a semi-successful business. Semi-successful because I still take on those handyman jobs to make ends meet.

I reach down and grab a couple. My bags sit where the waves of the Sound hit each shell, making them pristine when I pull them up. No need to power wash them to make them presentable. I like to mutter positive words in the presence of my bivalves, so I praise them for their strength and resilience, but my mind keeps going back to this morning.

I could kick myself for making those hearts on the window. It's my own damn fault. I just wanted to embarrass her, not let anyone think we were dating. I figured she was on some video with her book club, and they all know me, and they'd get a good laugh out of it. How was I supposed to know it was a bunch of strangers from the worst TV show in existence?

After that show tried to humiliate my sister, there's no way

I'd ever be involved with it. I mean, she won in the end by dating the greatest rockstar there is, but that show did nothing good for our family. Freaking *Love at the Last Resort*. I thought we were done with that garbage. I can't believe she wants to bring it here.

I separate some oysters into less populated bags. Measuring them in my mind, looking for the magic three-inch mark as I go. But I can't quite settle my thoughts, so I get out of the water, sit on the upside-down bucket next to the shack, and dial Ollie, my younger but sensible and rational brother. We're a close-knit family, with weekly family gatherings or video meetings and everyone up in each other's business. The angst I'm feeling can only be calmed by a conversation with a Sherman.

"Hey, bro," he answers on the first ring.

"How's the big city?"

"Same old, same old. Crunching numbers and training for my next tri."

Ollie is one of the most regimented people I know. It makes him a great accountant and fantastic athlete.

"Nice, proud of you."

"You should come into the city. Check out some bars with me. Be my wingman and see if we can find some dates."

Maybe I should move to the city and commute back to take care of my oysters so I don't have to deal with Tippy and her inane ideas.

"Sounds like a dream. If only..."

"How are things on good old Greensea?"

"Oysters are doing well. Mom and Dad are doing their thing."

"Good. Going to come over and work on Dad's taxes for the store in the next few days. Happy to take a quick look at yours too."

Our family owns the island's favorite store, Cedar & Fern. It resembles a ragtag fishing village: three clapboard buildings painted in various shades of green. Sells everything you might imagine, from groceries and gourmet pies to gardening items, clothing, and plants. We rent kayaks, paddle boards, and all the water equipment you could want. Dad loved handing over the bookkeeping to Oliver. Pretty handy to have an accountant in the family. For me, it means I can spend more time tending to my oysters and less time in front of the computer.

"Not like you to call out of the blue. What's up? Everything really okay?"

Oliver knows me too well.

"Sort of. Do you know what Tippy's trying to do?"

"Umm, why would I have any idea what Tippy Meadow-croft is doing? Trying to take over her dad's newspaper? Making a pitch to buy Cedar & Fern? Trying to rehab The Old Owl?"

"No! Bringing *Love at the Last Resort* to the island!"

Ollie says nothing for a few seconds.

"To Greensea?"

'Yes! To film on the island."

"Really...interesting," says Ollie. "No way it will happen."

"Have you met Tippy? Anything's possible with her in charge." Maybe he hasn't watched her as closely as I have over the years. He's younger, after all. Like, who would have thought there would be an exercise class on the old, rusty ferry that sits in Grays Bay? But thanks to Tippy, the Fit Greenies meet there once a month to practice their walking routines.

"The actual logistics it would take to run a show on Greensea are intense. From what I've seen, the numbers for *Love at the Last Resort* haven't been that great. So the network won't have the money to sink into the infrastructure they'd need to film on the island."

That's why I called Ollie. He deals in specifics and numbers. He would put the reality in reality TV.

"Plus, there's no way Mayor Nickerbottom will let some fancy TV show shack up on the island. Imagine all the annoying tourists and extra problems they'll bring."

"I don't know, bro. I think the mayor would love to have something like this here. Imagine how much money the tourists will bring," I point out.

"Right, the city may like it, but that doesn't equate to dollars for the network. You'd have to prove being on Greensea was better than, say, South Padre. I'm not sure any network exec would believe that."

I lean back against the shack. He has a point. I may be worrying about something that will never see the light of day.

"Well, that's not even the worst part."

"There's something worse than bringing reality TV to an island that is known for not having a single chain establishment on it?" Ollie asks.

"Yep."

He's never going to believe this.

"Okay. What?"

"Tippy told them we were dating, and now they want to see videos of us out on dates. And some bigwig producers are going to come out here to meet us."

Oliver's laugh is so loud I have to hold the phone away from my ear, and I'm convinced people across the bay can hear him too.

"It's not funny. I can't date Tippy Meadowcroft!"

"Chill out, bro! It's just a fake date. No one's asking you to marry her. But how the hell did this happen?"

I explain my stupid mistakes and prepare to never live them down.

"Epic. You know what they say about payback. Happy to throw you a bachelor party when it comes time."

I roll my eyes, hang up, and trudge back to the cottage.

I hoped I'd at least get some sympathy from Ollie. I know he's too busy crunching numbers in Seattle to care about anything like this, but after my pickleball meltdown, I knew there was no sense going to Josh with my problem. He'd say it served me right. And Jac is fawning over her rockstar. Ollie was my only hope, but he doesn't care about the predicament I find myself in. If I tell Mom and Dad, they'll ohh and ahh and say it's a great idea to fake date Tippy.

My dating history leaves something to be desired. The last serious relationship I had was with Naomi, a nurse in Seattle. Met her at a happy hour I went to with Ollie. We dated for a few months, ones without an R because you can't harvest oysters then. She wasn't willing to move to the island and add a thirty minute commute to both ends of her twelve-hour shift. I got where she was coming from, but my job and life are not portable. Can't grow oysters in the middle of a concrete jungle. I need to be on Greensea. So we broke up. And since then, I've only been on a date with a new first grade teacher and one of Quinn's servers at The Old Owl. So Mom would be thrilled to see me dating someone, fake or not.

Still, not enough of a reason for this to happen.

I crack open a can of Coke. Too early for the beer I want to grab. The windows are open and a sea breeze blows in. I love sea air. If I could live outside, I might. Jac likes to say my house is only suitable for three seasons because of my open window habits. You just have to dress appropriately and know to close them when the tide's low.

I wander back down to the shack to throw my recycled oyster shells back on the shoreline and finish my other tasks for the day, hoping to set aside my problems.

CHAPTER SEVEN

I grab Bear, a Christmas present from Mom and Dad last year, and get him ready to head out on our crusade. He's my plus one at the moment and he couldn't be happier about it.

I want all the things. The family. Kids. And I want it on Greensea. Which makes it extra hard. Dating on an island is next to impossible. At least bringing the show to our island will increase the dating pool significantly...I hope. Until then, Bear's the love of my life.

I set him in the basket and wrap his green gingham leash around Bertha's handlebars. Misty rain still hangs in the air. The trees are cloaked with an early fog as the March sun doesn't rise high enough to burn it off. But the weather doesn't bother me. I just dress for it. I have a full rain suit for bike riding when needed. Of course, all of it's reflective too. Today I only need my rain jacket.

It took all my energy not to chase after Dave right away. Instead, I did all the chores in the house and dillydallied for as long as I could.

Dave's standing in his shack when I pull up. Dressed in his waders and a white t-shirt. I put my kickstand down and get off my bike, undoing my helmet straps and shaking out my hair.

"I could hear the wicked witch's theme song as you rode up." Dave tucks his escaping bangs underneath his knit hat. "All you need are some striped socks to go along with your getup."

I roll my eyes. His words are like water off a duck's back. They just roll off every time.

"I think you were exceeding the speed limit," he says, trying to get my goat again.

"Joke's on you. This fine bicycle can't go any faster than the island limit. I programmed the motor so it won't go above it."

Some people hack their e-bikes to go faster, but I slowed mine down. I have no intention of getting a speeding ticket while I'm riding my bike around.

"You're the only person I know brave enough to wear white leggings on a bike ride to an oyster shack."

White's my signature color, regardless of what may happen.

"First, I'm not planning on getting dirty. Second, they're not leggings, Dave. They're joggers. And, they're ecru."

Nothing, not even the unpredictable weather in the PNW, will make me give up wearing fashionable athleisure wear. Plus, they have a reflective stripe down the side to help drivers see me. If eye rolls had a sound, I'd be able to hear Dave's rattle around from here.

"What's up? Why are you here? Getting down on one knee to propose?"

I let Bear run around while I stick my bike helmet in my basket and walk up to the shack.

"No. I'm here to plan the dates we need to send into the producers."

"You're kidding, right? You know I'm not doing this. I said no."

"You have to do it. They think we're together."

Dave messes with some shells, moving them from one bucket to another behind the counter. He doesn't make any eye contact. He's serious. Shit. What if he won't do it? I take a bunch of my hair and start braiding it, my nervous habit, the one I used to break me of biting my fingernails.

"Find yourself another faker. It will not happen, and no one on this island would ever believe we were on a date to begin with."

"I don't need anyone on the island to think we're on a date, I just need the TV people to think that we're a couple."

First idea...ignore his misgivings and start planning anyway.

"Okay. Our first date will be at The Old Owl. Nice casual setting. Great view of the harbor. We can play darts. Easy banter and done."

"Not going to happen." Dave sets down a bucket, and a bunch of sea slop splatters at my feet.

"Gross. Keep your slime to yourself, and of course it's going to happen."

I grab Bear as he's about to lick some of the slop up. I read somewhere that shellfish carry disgusting diseases.

"Me plus you is not an equation that exists." He grabs a shell out of the bucket, holds it to eye level, and examines it.

"Dude, we're not in middle school anymore. I'm not carving *TL4E* into a tree."

"Never could figure out what that meant," he says.

"True love forever, bozo."

The conversation is saved by someone who pulls up in an old Subaru. At least I have a minute to think and come up with a new plan.

"Hey, Sam," says Dave. "Got your dozen right here."

Dave hands him a bag of shells. Someone else out on a walk with their dog approaches and asks Dave for a dozen too. This place is busy. It's a glorified lemonade stand. Imagine what it could be if he put a little elbow grease into it. Some tables. White lights. Make the shack a little bigger. The place has potential. Especially if people want to come here to buy buckets of goop.

That's when all of my light bulbs turn on.

"These things are pretty popular?" I ask.

"They're not things. Oysters are bivalve mollusks. They're saving the world..."

He's going to go on and on, so I cut him off.

"Save it. I'm going to make you a deal. What if I help you get this place in order?" I point to the shack. "We'll put up some tables. Make it a proper destination."

He stares at me. "You think you can bribe me to date you?"

"I wouldn't call it a bribe. It's a deal. We could put it in writing if you'd like. Make it official."

Dave rubs his chin and looks around the place. I may have found his weak spot. This idea might work. A coat of paint will do wonders for this little shack.

"I'd need more than that."

He's using dirty used-car salesman tactics with my life.

"More than that? Are you kidding me? I'm single-handedly trying to turn your business around and make it into something."

"It's already something. I don't need your help to do that." He turns around and keeps working in his buckets.

"But I can help make it bigger. Better." I think for a second. What else can I do to help him? "Would this be a good time for me to remind you that this is all your fault? I was doing fine on my Zoom call before you started making gestures behind me. If you'd kept those to yourself, none of this would have happened."

Dave pretends he doesn't hear me. He takes a rake from

inside the shack starts pushing around the muck closer to the shoreline.

I fling out ideas.

"I'll get my dad to run a full page for Sherman Shellfish. The *Gazette* will offer free advertising."

He keeps pushing muck.

"We'll give you a platform to talk about how you're saving the world with those things."

Another push with the rake.

"Photos. Graphs. A monthly column of things people can do to save the shoreline."

If he doesn't take me up on my offer soon, owning the paper will be on the table before you know it.

He thinks again, walks back to the shack, and returns the rake. Then he takes his knit hat off and runs his hands through his hair. "I would like the publicity."

"See!" Bingo! "It's a win-win for both of us." I knew there'd be some way to convince Dave to do this.

"But!" He points his finger in the air like Magellan just discovered a new land.

And I knew there'd be a but. What else does he want? Blood?

"We need a set of ground rules."

"Ground rules? I won't paint the place pink or anything."

"I'm not talking about for that. I mean for our fake date."

Good point. We will need some rules. "What did you have in mind?"

"You're paying for the date."

This time I roll my eyes.

"Any touching will be for the camera, and you cannot get mad at me for anything I do."

"We don't have to touch." Gross. Touching Dave is like petting an ugly dog.

"How are you going to convince them it's real if we don't even touch?"

Two minutes ago he didn't want to pretend to date me, and now he's talking about touching? But he has a good point.

"Okay. Hands can touch. Arms are okay. Low back if necessary. That should be enough."

"Good. No kissing," he adds.

"Of course not!" This isn't "The Frog Prince." No chance of my kissing him and turning him into a prince.

But shoot. The producers need to believe he's my prince. I need to sell this. They need to believe these places are perfect for dates. How am I going to do that with someone like Dave? I pace back and forth. My plan is falling apart with every step forward.

"You're going to get your ecru all dirty if you keep moving like that."

"I take it back. We might have to kiss to make this believable."

He thinks about it. Looks like he might throw up as he looks around the shack. "Only if necessary."

"Can we shake on the one date and day with the producers?" I stretch my hand out.

"Deal. In exchange for all the things you mentioned."

I need to think. Be on my own. Work on the rest of the plan.

"I'll be in touch."

First round goes to Tippy, even though my stomach turns every time I think about having to pretend Dave's my boyfriend. If I'd acted faster, this all could have been avoided, but instead I'm going to be exchanging friendship bracelets, and maybe a little spit, with none other than Dave Sherman. I put on my helmet, pop Bear back in the basket, get on my bike, and head home.

When I get home, Mom's setting up the flower stand at the end of the driveway. It's an island favorite, Bell's Blooms. She's putting out some early daffodils in little jars. Branches from a few trees dotted with little buds. She sets them up each morning before she heads to her store on Main Street. People use the honor system and put money in the box. In all the years she's been doing this, I think she's only lost three vases worth of flowers. Sometimes the honesty on this island slays me.

"Looks good, Mom!"

"Thanks, sweets. Where are you coming from?"

"Just a little ride around. Nowhere in particular." I shrug and blow it off.

"Sounds nice, sweetie." Mom gives me a once over. "You have that I'm-on-a-mission-glow."

I haven't told anyone, not even Sylviane, about my idea to bring *Love at the Last Resort* to the island. I'm not sure Mom and Dad will understand. I need to get all my ducks in a row and perfect my sales pitch before I tell them what I'm up to.

I hop off my bike and arrange a few branches in an empty vase. "I've got a few things turning in my mind. Nothing concrete yet."

Mom nods. "Want to come to the store with me today?"

"Thanks, but I need to work on my column and get a few things done around here."

We continue to work quietly making the perfect bouquets. Just being around Mom relaxes me. For as long as I can remember, she's been the hostess with the mostest. She's always thrown elaborate dinner parties. Her themes are obscure little celebrations of things you may have missed. Like a blackberry party the day the berries were ripe. Table decorated in deep purples and reds. Foods served with berries inside of them or on top. Solar eclipse called for a half-moon party. Everything she served was in a crescent shape, just the way the sun looked. And always a gorgeous table. Her tables put anything you find on Pinterest to shame. Hers are creative and eye popping. She gained a name from them, and the rest is history.

Years ago, she did what many housewives on Greensea do: she opened a store on Main Street. Hers was a tablescapes store. She sells everything you could need to make your table look great...except dishes and silverware. So, pretty much just the extras. Like rattan chargers to sit under your plates. Napkin rings in the shape of flowerpots. Ceramic seasonal animals. Vessels for centerpieces. Nature's incorporated into every one of her tablescapes. So many of the flowers she uses are from our gardens. Gardens she's had forever. She's always out digging in her overalls, dirt under her nails and caked on her gardening shoes. Rehoming slugs like it's her business. Planting bulbs in pouring rain. Covering buds before the last frost. Bell is not a delicate flower. She contains multitudes.

She's full service in everything she does. Including being a mom. She never sat us in front of a television. She made home-made playdough, Barbie houses from boxes. She found a way to entertain us, even when money was tight.

Mom fills the last vase and wipes her hands on her pants.

"Whatever's got you so quiet must be a doozy, dear. Hope you're using your power for something good." She laughs.

I sure hope so too. Bell Meadowcroft has set a walk-through-the-world-with-poise-and-kindness bar so high I don't know what else I can do to live up to it. The worst part about all of it is that Topper and Bell have never once pressured me to do anything other than what I want to do, except to be kind. I am the ultimate poster child for well-adjusted parenting. Topper and Bell are role model parents, the kind who support their kids in whatever they do, whether it be an academic scholarship to an elite college or first place in summer camp wheelbarrow races. And all I want to do is something amazing that will let them know I appreciate them and all they've done. Bringing *Love at the Last Resort* to Greensea will do that because one: huge win. Two: the revenues it will bring to the paper and the entire island will be substantial. I'll be helping the family business in more ways than anyone can imagine. It's the least I can do for them after what they've given me. Maybe they can finally think about retiring. Three: (My brain's put this as three, but maybe it's number one.) It will drive up the bachelor pool on the island, and maybe even I will find love.

Mom walks to her Wagoneer. "Oh! Don't forget to call or text Simon. It's his birthday today!"

I pull out my phone and do it before I forget.

My brother Simon is off in New York running a successful financial company. He deals in mergers and acquisitions for forward-thinking environmental companies, because it's not enough to just run a successful company; Simon needs to make the world a better place too. And me, I write a gossip column. I need to step it up. I need to get to the tippy top. And find a partner to go with me.

Greensea was never enough for Simon. He felt smothered by small-town island life. So he moved to another island, similar in size but opposite in every way: Manhattan. He pops in for forty-eight hours at Christmas and says his door is always open when we make the trip out east. But otherwise we're not that close. The Sherman siblings make me jealous. They move as a pack. I'm sure they have a secret family bat signal that lights up in the sky when one of them is in trouble. When Nick left Jac, it was a full-court rescue operation to make sure she felt supported on all fronts. Then the way they supported her when she started dating Johnny Nickel was inspiring. Dave, Josh, and Ollie made sure he was on the up-and-up. Now I've watched them embrace

Sylviane, an almost orphan of a person, and support her in every way. It's remarkable, and I'm envious of the sibling relationships they seem to have. Dave and Josh have battled it out over the years, but it's been a good-hearted ribbing more than anything else. Maybe someday, Simon and I will be back to that. Maybe he'll see my worth when I bring the TV show here.

GREENSEA GAZETTE

Islanders,

Thanks to Mayor Nickerbottom, Greensea has a new contest—a seagull-calling contest. What a great idea to introduce something that causes people as much pain as a fourth grade recorder concert. This writer would like to suggest placing all the contestants in the high school gymnasium and letting them practice there instead of letting the sounds echo through island homes. You have neighbors, people! Isn't the incessant cock-a-doodle-doo of the rooster enough? (Watch the ballot box for a city ordinance on that one!)

With the change in season, it's time to shake things up over here. As more people move to the island and our population increases, it's harder and harder for GG to keep up on all the news. So we've created a spot on our homepage for you to submit your stories. Anonymously, of course! Tell us every juicy detail of what you see, everything you hear in the grocery line, and especially every tale from the ferry. Remember, people aren't necessarily interested in what you're doing, they're more interested in what you're hiding. Share away, people of Greensea! Share away!

XOXO,

GG

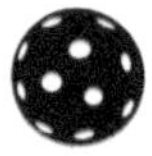

TIPPY

There are few things I love more than a fresh manicure and pedicure, but the only place on Greensea is all organic. Yes, I love that the color I put on my nails doesn't seep extra chemicals into my body, but I swear it's a business gimmick because the stuff peels off right away, making it necessary to come back sooner than you want. Unless, of course, you buy one of their homemade polishes to do your own touch-ups, and if you know me, you know that's what I do.

Sylviane pulls into the parking lot at the same time I do.

"Hey, girl!" I say as she gets out of her car. We've only known each other for a few months, since she inherited her uncle's cabin. Some may say we're an unlikely pairing. Very Laverne and Shirley. But it works for us. She keeps me honest and helps me see things in a different light. Fresh perspective is not a bad thing, just something I can choose to ignore if I'd like. She's the only person who will tell me what they think of my new plan and my current dilemma.

"How's it going?" Sylviane tucks a stray blonde hair behind her ear and closes her car door.

I walk over and grab her arm. "Great." I giggle a little because I can't wait to tell her about my plan.

We walk into ANN's All Natural Nails Salon. Ann, salon owner, nail aficionado, and self-proclaimed wordsmith, greets us from her spot on a low, rolling stool. Besides glamming up nails (naturally, of course), Ann loves anything and everything to do with words. The alliteration she's used in naming her organic polish colors is second to none. *Greensea Gull*, a subtle light gray. *Dill of a Day*, green, naturally. *It's Better at Bungalow Bay*, shimmering aquamarine. And she will most definitely ask us if we've done the Wordle today.

Sylviane picks a clear polish.

"No way. You have to do something more exciting than that."

She rolls her eyes and picks up a yellowy peachy coral called *Golden Hour for the Golden Girl*.

"Satisfied?"

"Better." I pick *Strawberry Sash*, and Ann shows us to the pedicure chairs.

"We didn't get to talk at pickleball after Dave's monster meltdown. What's up with you? How's Josh?"

Sylviane and Josh moved in together not too long ago. They're the latest island ferry tale, the mapmaker and the magician. They fell for each other while they put together the annual Harvest Fest. Their love story is about as Greensea as it gets.

Sylviane's cheeks turn the color of my polish. "He's good. I'm just doing the final proof of the new book and trying to sort out what the next will be."

Turns out Sylviane's uncle was the author of a series of cozy mysteries, and she's taken over since he passed away.

I slap my hands on my legs. That's about as much time as I

can waste without telling her my news. "Okay. Enough about you. I'm dying to tell someone what I did."

Ann's turned the water on for both of our feet to soak. I lean in close so no one can hear us over the rush of the water.

"I entered Greensea into a contest," I say in my lowest voice.

"What kind of contest?" Sylviane asks.

"Have you heard of the show *Love at the Last Resort*?"

"I think Josh mentioned it. Wasn't his brother-in-law on it?"

"Yes, he was. Although, technically he and Jac weren't married when he was on the show. Anyway, they're scouting new locations for the next season."

"And..." Sylviane prompts.

"And I think Greensea is the perfect destination for them."

"What makes you think Greensea would be a suitable spot for a reality TV show?"

Is she crazy? I shouldn't need to explain this to her. I pull my foot away from Ann in shock. Ann grabs it back and holds it in a tighter grip.

"Greensea is the quintessential location. We couldn't be more picturesque. We have ferry rides galore. We're mentioned in Johnny Nickel's hit song. We have the cutest Main Street in America. A bookstore named Between the Covers, for goodness' sake. We're practically begging to be the next venue for their show."

"Have you talked to any of the Shermans about this? I imagine they might not love the idea, given the history they have with it."

"Yes," I say and get ready to tell her the next part. "Dave and I are even pretending to date for the show."

"WHAT?!" Sylviane's eyes grow to the size of pickleballs. "After the disaster on the court, he agreed to work with you?"

"Yeah, well, things happened, and, well," I stammer while I sugarcoat the truth. "Dave and I are going out on a date!"

Sylviane looks to the side and wrinkles her forehead, questioning me. Then she shakes her head.

"I don't want to know. Whatever you're up to has to have two sides. I don't want to be tainted by only hearing yours."

"This is not a sides thing. We all have one common goal—bring *Love at the Last Resort* to Greensea."

Sylviane gives me another look and lets out a giggle as they buff her ticklish feet.

"You and Dave have spoken about this?"

"Of course we have!" That's the truth. She doesn't need to know about our deal.

Ann's holding my foot still as she uses the pumice stone. Being ticklish plus aggravated means I'm extra hard to keep still today.

Sylviane studies my face like she can find the truth somewhere behind my willow-colored foundation.

"What did you have to do to get Dave Sherman to agree to date you?"

Forgot. Sylviane's a reporter. She's excellent at asking the direct questions to make sure no one's lying.

"I didn't have to do anything. Yet."

She raises her eyebrows and I spill the beans without hesitation.

"Ugh. Okay. I'm going to give the oyster shack a glow up in exchange for his cooperation." I spit it out as fast as I can. If I'm pretending to date Dave, I'm going to need to hold onto the truth a little bit better.

"Just be careful. Don't mess around with people. Especially with *Love at the Last Resort* involved. The show may look back at the history of everything that happened with Jac. It may drag up some bad memories."

"Give me a break. Jac's with the hottest rockstar in the world. She couldn't care less about what happens on this little reality show. And, don't forget, she came out smelling like a rose!"

This is supposed to be my grand gesture to Greensea. Can't she see that?

"Tell me about the process."

"Well, I sent in a proposal and Greensea made it to the next step. Dave and I are going to go on a date, send in another video, and then some producers are coming to the island to check out the locations. I'm hoping that will be all they need to crown us the winner."

Meeting them in person will seal the deal. As soon as they see my effervescent personality and the cinematic backdrop of Greensea, they'll have to bring the show here.

"I bet there will be many people on Greensea who will have some feelings about a reality show being filmed on the island. Greensea residents seem to have a lot of opinions."

Sylviane's right, but I plan to turn the tide in my GG columns. She's the only one, other than Mom and Dad, who knows I write the columns. I have to imagine half the island could figure it out if they spent any time on it, but no one cares enough. It took Sylviane about three minutes to put two and two together and track me down, but no one wants to upset the column. GG has been around for a long time. It's an institution. Outing GG would be tantamount to telling a bunch of preschoolers that Santa isn't real. People ignore what they don't want to know.

"I'll handle the opinions when it comes to that. I have to get through our first date before I can do anything else."

"I know you'll shine in whatever you end up doing."

She's right. I always end up coming out on top because I work on controlling everything to make sure there's no other outcome.

"Let's get back to you and Dave. I don't understand what's

going on between you two. He helped you up when you fell over at the dessert dash. Why'd you two act like idiots at pickleball?"

True. Dave helped me up at Harvest Fest, but he put a little whipped cream in my ear while I was trying to stand up. He could've left me, but he saw an opportunity to make my situation worse and took it.

"Oh, you know when you grow up with someone and they've been teasing you for decades? He put gum in my hair. Put an *I love Thomas* sign on my back when I had a crush in sixth grade and I didn't want it advertised to the entire school."

"Sounds like he was a brat, but I'm sure you didn't take it sitting down."

"Yeah, you're right. I taped him into a box one time during recess, but that's on him because who's dumb enough to crawl into a box when I'm standing around? But it's like we never grew up. Both back here after college. Now when I see him at The Old Owl, he does stupid crap like buying a drink for a guy at the bar and saying it's from me."

"You know, they say the person who teases you likes you." Sylviane quirks an eyebrow.

My parents and my teachers have repeated that line for decades. It's not the case anymore. That's for sure.

"They say that when you're six, not when you're my age. And this is more like we're both bored from living on an island. Not enough people around here some days."

"I guess the truth will come out when you start dating."

Sylviane winks, and I let the whir of the massage chair walk away with my thoughts.

GREENSEA GAZETTE

Has this become the Island of Misfits and Misfit Toys? And no, I don't mean the sweet Christmas tale where everything turns out alright. City council is implementing new outrageous "traffic calming" measures and have they ever gotten creative. Have you been down Pineapple Cove Drive? The clowns have created a virtual obstacle course. Four-foot metal posts every six feet marking the lanes on all sides, including the middle. The intersection of Pineapple Cove and Cherry Street has a roundabout made out of the same posts. We've never seen anything like it. Poor Mr. Jackson's horse reins got stuck on the monstrosity and nearly catapulted him from the carriage. Plan to leave extra travel time if you dare to attempt the new drive. But never fear, we have been told by some smart teenagers that it only takes a little bit of practice to go through and maintain your drag-racing speed. And kudos to Mr. Wells for taking the Greensea Dog Agility team out there to practice! At least the border collies on the island are happy with the new addition! We can't wait to see *how the snow plows make their way down the street during the first snowstorm of the season.*

XOXO,

GG

CHAPTER NINE

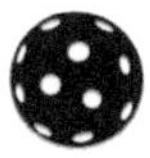

Tippy arrives in Topper's pickup at eight AM to start the glow up. She sent me a brief text telling me to clear my morning but didn't give any clues about her plans for my business.

Today she's dressed in all black. Definitely a better color for what's ahead of us. She pulls out a plywood sign from the back of the truck. It's white with *Sherman's Shellfish* meticulously hand-painted in blue-green. Why hadn't I ever thought of that before?

"Like it?" she asks.

"Yeah. If that's a clue to what you have in mind for this place, it might not be all bad."

Tippy grabs four cans of paint, paintbrushes, a tool bag, and cleaning supplies out of the truck. You name it, she has it.

"You know, I have some stuff of my own."

"Dave Sherman, I don't know what you have, so I came prepared."

Tippy's assumed her hands-on-her-hips pose. If she weren't

a good six inches shorter than I am, I'd think she was looking down her nose at me.

"Two picnic tables will be delivered around eleven. I think they should go about here."

Tippy walks to the grassy area between the shoreline and the road.

"Okay," I say. General Meadowcroft has reported for duty.

"Tide never comes up here, does it?"

"Nah. Not unless there's a tsunami. Probably have bigger things to worry about in that case."

Josh has warned me, with all his fancy maps, that this is a flood plain in the event of a tsunami. I get it. I appreciate it. And I don't care. I may run out and save my little creatures if there is one, but I will not worry about the shack or my cottage withstanding a wall of water. I can make my way to higher ground if need be.

"What color are you planning on painting this thing?" I tilt my head in the direction of the shack. Most people would have consulted with their "client" regarding things like paint color. But not Tippy.

"Red with white trim. The red will pop against the green trees, and the sign plays off the color of the bay."

"Red? Not usually a fan."

"It's a power color, Dave. Teams dressed in red perform better in sporting events. It's the color of generals and warriors."

Surprised she's not wearing it all the time then but I suppose it's built in with her hair.

"In case you didn't notice, this is an oyster shack. Not any of those things."

Tippy doesn't listen. Instead she lays a drop cloth around the foundation. But before we do anything more than set up, a green Lincoln Town Car pulls up, and I know we're in trouble. Mayor Nickerbottom.

He gets out of the car, tips his newsboy cap toward Tippy, and beelines right for me.

"Hello, Dave. I came to inspect your permits."

Shit. I didn't even think about that. "It's just a little glow up, Mayor. No need for paperwork."

"Now, Dave. You know there's no such thing as a glow up without paperwork on Greensea Island. To start, let's look at the size of your sign." Mayor Nickerbottom pulls a tape measure out of his back pocket.

"Hello, Mayor Nickerbottom! Give me a second. I have everything you need right here." Tippy goes to the truck and pulls out a clipboard. "Let's see. Feel free to measure the sign, but you'll see it falls well within the city guidelines. The letters are three and 7/8 inches wide as required. I have the permit to add seating to the bank right here. Here's the permit to serve food on the premises. And here's the necessary food safety paperwork. As you can see, the utility company came out and marked the underground utilities so we can place a post to string lights."

How did I not notice the markings on the ground?

Mayor Nickerbottom smiles. "Tippy, you have your mom's genes. I believe you've taken care of everything. Dave, I hope you thank this young woman. I sure don't know why she'd help you like this."

I put my hands in my pockets. "I'm not sure why either."

I squint my eyes and give her a closer look. Why is this so important to her? The mayor gets back in his car and pulls away.

"What gives? Why are you doing all of this for me?"

"You know why! I need you to pretend to be my date."

"Yeah, but why is *Love at the Last Resort* so important to you?"

"I just want it to happen. Okay, Dave?"

She stiffens up and grabs a paintbrush and a paint can

opener to pry open a lid. She's done talking. Her hair's tied back in a long braid, but a few curls escape around her face. When Tippy sets her mind to something, there's no stopping her. Clearly.

"What do you want me to do?" I ask.

"Grab a paintbrush and get to work."

I take one of the brushes she brought over and work on the front of the shack.

"This would've been easier with a roller."

"Not on wood like this. We'd still have to cover it with a brush. The bristles get into the little crevices." She's right. Of course.

The sun's shining and there's a hint of spring in the air. I grab my phone out of my pocket and turn on a playlist. It'll make the silence less awkward. For the first time in maybe forever, I'm not compelled to mock her or fight with Tippy and it's freaking me out.

"Thanks for doing this," I say.

"Thanks for agreeing to be my date," she says.

We've set a record for the time we've been in each other's presence and not tormented one another. We might pull this stunt off after all.

"What do you have in mind for dates?"

"I have a list in my notebook. I'll show you when we take a break."

Of course she has a list. Probably wrote a novel. A dissertation on the best places to go on the island. One thing about Tippy is she's a hard worker. She busts her ass getting things done and right now, when the thing is my oysters, we're benefitting from her tenacity.

We finish painting the outside of the shack red, and we begin painting white on the inside, starting with the ceiling. Tippy's on the five-foot ladder and I'm on a step stool, each working toward the center. The ceiling's the worst part. Staring up with your neck tilted back. Painful, and we shouldn't have saved it for the end. We're close enough that our heads bump. And then I feel something brush my hair.

"Oh my gosh! I'm so sorry."

I jump off the stool and feel the top of my head. "What the heck, Tip?" My hand's covered in *Magnolia White* paint. I run out to Topper's truck to have a look in the side-view mirror. I've aged thirty years. I'm my dad. Worse yet, I'm Grandpa Sherman.

Tippy runs up next to me. "I'm so sorry. I didn't mean to get your head! I just reached back, and it happened."

I eye her. "You did this on purpose." I grit my teeth, ready to take her on. I could grab a paintbrush. Paint some of her long hair right at the root like she did to me.

"I did not do it on purpose! I need you to be camera ready. I wouldn't do anything to jeopardize that."

True. She wouldn't mess with our fake date, that's one thing I know for sure.

"Does paint come out with shampoo?"

Tippy bites her lip. "Umm...This kind might not?"

"Clearly that means no. Of all the things you could have done."

I run my hands through my hair, hoping I can still get some of the wet paint out, to no avail.

"It was an accident. I swear."

"Well, I guess you had to one-up me after I interrupted your meeting didn't you? Joke's on you though, because it appears we can only go places where I can wear a hat."

"Or you can get a buzz cut."

"I'm not getting a freaking buzz cut, Tippy." I love my hair. I don't know what I'd do if I couldn't do my signature head flip to get my hair out of my eyes.

A Prius pulls up, the official car of Greensea Island—especially the Sherman family, and I realize Ollie must have finished his work with Dad early. Glad he's here, because I might need someone to make sure I don't give Tippy's curls their own frosted tips.

"Well, well, well. What do we have here?" he asks as he gets out of the car.

"Tippy 'accidentally' painted my head. Or so she says."

"Hi, Tippy. Long time no see." Ollie walks toward the enemy.

"Hey, Ollie."

He gives her a hug. None of the rivalry that Tippy and I have carries over to my other siblings. They're all happy-go-lucky around her, and it infuriates me.

"What'd you do to deserve that?" Oliver points to my head.

"Believe it or not, not one thing." For the first time in forever, I didn't deserve it.

"You guys go do your brother thing. I'll finish up out here, Dave. It's the least I can do," says Tippy, grabbing her brush.

"Sure is," I mumble as Ollie and I walk across the street to the house.

I head straight to the bathroom to get a better look than Topper's truck allowed me. Somehow, she painted a huge stripe. Worse than a skunk. Down my entire head and about a quarter of an inch from my scalp, requiring a complete shaving of my head to take care of it. I love my hair. I'm the only one in my family with board straight brown hair. I love how it swoops down over my eyebrows. Shines like I'm in a shampoo commercial. And bounces with every step. It's my best feature. And now I need to get rid of it.

"Yo, Ollie," I yell. "I'm going to jump in the shower and see if any of this will come out. You good?"

"Yeah. I'll catch up on emails."

Even though I know a shower won't help, it's worth a try anyway. I empty most of the bottle of shampoo into my hand and lather it up like nobody's business. I am not getting a buzz cut. No way. No how. There's got to be some sort of hack on the internet to get paint out of hair.

"Any luck?" Ollie asks as I open the door.

"No."

"Come on over, Gramps. What was going on out there anyway?" Ollie asks.

"I told you. Tippy painted my head."

"No, I mean, it felt like more than a fake dating scenario."

"It's not more than anything, except an annoyance." Fake dating Tippy is already causing me issues.

"Well, you're going to be quite a sight for those dates."

I take a baseball cap off the hook by the front door, grab my notebook, and throw it on the table.

"Here are all my figures. It's pretty straightforward." I sit down across from him.

Ollie opens the book. "So you want to grow the business?"

"Yes. Oyster farming is actually a sustainable..."

"I know the spiel. You don't have to convince me. I'll see what the numbers say."

I've been contemplating taking out a small business loan to cover my expansion. I'd love to add oysters to different parts of the Sound. Maybe even get a boat so I can place some cages out farther in the water. Maybe hire an employee. More oysters equal more positive impact on the environment. Before I apply for the loan, I want to make sure it's a solid idea and I can handle repayment. The mortgage on the house is low. The income I already bring in from the oysters plus my work as a handyman around the island should be enough. Almost every islander I know has multiple jobs. If you live and work on the island, there are very few things that pay enough money to afford to live on Greensea. Let's face it, our groceries aren't cheap. We pay a premium for island living, and Greensea doesn't have corporate jobs. Most bigwigs commute into the city every day, but that's not for me. I'm all smiles making my way on my own around here.

"Mind logging into your bank account so I can see what you have? Your numbers are pretty clean on this side."

Ollie isn't like me. He wanted all the trappings of the corporate lifestyle. The regular paycheck and hours. I've never been called to that kind of monotony.

I grab my laptop and log in.

"Gonna send the Meadowcrofts a bill for pain and suffering from all this, so my bottom line will be a little bigger soon."

Ollie shakes his head and looks at my account.

CHAPTER TEN

TIPPY

Before I leave Sherman's Shellfish, I take some pictures. The fresh red paint pops against the cloudy backdrop and the dark green trees. This could be something if Dave invested some actual money into it. Maybe he could get a liquor license. It's a place the diner guy on TV would visit. The picnic tables fit perfectly between the shack and the shoreline. The lights hang from the temporary pole I've placed in a pot. I wanted Dave to know what it would look like to stay in my good graces, but I can't dig a hole and place a pole in cement on my own. A temporary solution is the best answer for today.

The steps creak as I walk up the porch to pry Dave out of the house, prompting him to meet me at the screen door.

"You don't have anything in your hands, do you?"

I put them both up. "I come in peace."

He walks out onto the porch.

"Walk down to the shack and check it out before I go."

His hat's covering my mistake. I'm sure Glenda at Greensea Glam could fix him up in no time if need be.

We walk down the steps in silence, cross the street, and stand in front of Sherman's Shellfish. Dave doesn't say a word, just stands with his arms crossed turning in a complete circle giving it all a once over. I try to get clues from his face but he stays silent with his lips pursed in the same position, guarding all of his emotions.

In the meantime, Oliver's joined us on the grass.

"You've outdone yourself, Tip! Hope you took some before and afters, because this is amazing." At least one Sherman brother has a glowing review.

Dave shakes his head. "Not bad. Not bad at all."

"What do you mean, not bad? This place just went from rundown to destination on the rating scale of Greensea locations," I plead.

"Don't mind him," says Oliver. "The paint's messing with his brain."

I gather most of my stuff and sling it into Dad's truck. "Since we didn't discuss the rest of our plans, I'll need you at Meadowcroft in an hour."

"You know I have a life, right? Like I can't just put everything aside because you want to get this TV show, right?"

"You took care of your little creatures. What else is there to do?"

Oliver stands like he's watching a game of pickleball, his head turning between us.

"Um...paperwork. This is an actual business. Just because you've got your dad taking care of everything for you doesn't mean everyone else does."

"My dad?" I put my hands on my hips.

"Yeah, Topper. About yay tall." He holds up his hands to his chin.

"I know who you're talking about, Dave, but my dad doesn't take care of things for me. Neither does my mom."

"I'd say there was some privilege that helped you get your house."

"You mean because my grandma died and left it to me?"

He interrupts. "It's a privilege to be left a house."

"And now I work at the paper, teach Fit Greenies classes, and give pickleball lessons to afford all the upkeep on the court and my house. My parents don't give handouts."

He rolls his eyes. "There's a lot of privilege in each of those jobs."

My face turns red. My head feels like it's going to explode. "There's a lot of inherent privilege living on an island, but I've never rested on my laurels. I had to replace the heat pump and several windows last year, so I covered recess at Grays Bay Elementary to boost my income. I'm always trying to make money and trying new things. What do you think I'm doing with this new plan?" I take a deep breath. "Give me a break! I'm not a millennial with a trust fund grifting on Greensea in Daddy's summerhouse."

Why can't he see I'm the Energizer bunny? Always moving at a quick clip. And never sitting at Wine Down eating fancy olives and an expensive charcuterie.

"Apologies. You are an enterprising young dame." He tips his baseball cap to me.

"I'm not a character from a 1950s family comedy either. I'm thirty-two, you know. Just like you."

I pick up the last of my things and throw them into the truck. Clap my hands together and wipe the sweat off my forehead.

"He'll be at your house tomorrow after he takes care of the oysters," offers Oliver.

Dave gives him a death stare.

"I'll be back from Pilates at ten. See you then."

As I get in the car, I hear Oliver say, "After she did all this, fake dating her is the least you can do."

I'm exhausted when I get home, but completing a project like that gives me a natural high. I run a bath filled with Epsom salts and wash off all the grime of the day. I slip into some lounge clothes and spread out at the dining room table with all my papers, pens, and materials. Time to plan the crap out of our date day with the producer.

I start with a list of all the places we need to take them. I need to highlight the beauty of Greensea, which is easy, but also capitalize on its most marketable characteristics. The popularity of pickleball makes it a no-brainer. It's the fastest growing sport and has garnered attention from all areas of the globe, even the Olympics.

The only problem is that Dave is hopeless at it. I'll have to give him a brief lesson so we don't blow the whole thing on the court. That's a problem for tomorrow.

Right now, I need to write my column and begin Operation-Get-Dave's-Business-Attention!

GREENSEA GAZETTE

Have you seen Sherman's Shellfish Shack? More importantly, did you see who was working on it together? Tippy Meadowcroft and Dave Sherman. Let's see who can be the first to get us the skinny on that duo. Last we saw, they were at odds with each other. I seem to remember a little kerfuffle over a shopping cart not too long ago. Anyway, stop in and try Dave's famous pearl producing bounty of the sea. You won't be disappointed!

In school news, it seems those PTO moms have an ax to grind with someone or someones. During Teacher Appreciation Week, the PTO crew went above and beyond for the teacher luncheon. The buffet table was set and salads were displayed with every-thing you can imagine for a salad bar of the nth degree... edamame, snap peas, iceberg to arugula (including kale, of course), grilled meats, beans, tofu, cheese, carrots. You name it, it was there. And the flowers were over the top. As the teachers went through the salad line, one of them noticed little flags in the centerpieces. She figured it was artwork and words of gratitude, as it was Teacher Appreciation Week. Upon closer inspection, it appeared they were declarations about the women of the PTO. And none of them too flattering. One read, Down With Blondes! *Another read,* PTO Moms Need A Real Job. *A third,* Helicopter Somewhere Else. *No one knows who placed these special messages in the arrangements. Surely none of the people who were there would have done such a thing, or would they? Did someone steal the oh-so-coveted PTO presidency from someone else?*

XOXO,

GG

CHAPTER ELEVEN

TIPPY

I hear the muffler on Dave's truck before I see him coming down the driveway. At least he's on time.

"How'd the Sherman's Shellfish makeover look this morning?"

"Had to wear sunglasses to shield my eyes from the red, but otherwise I have to admit it looked pretty good."

"Hmph." I shake my head. The next thing I'll have to glow up is his car. I make a mental note to find him one he can borrow when the producer is here. And then I'll work on his wardrobe.

"The know-it-all GG saw it too," he says.

"Oh yeah?" I play dumb.

"Somehow they even knew we worked on it together."

"GG knows everything."

I walk toward the court.

"I have half a mind to think Mayor Nickerbottom's writing that garbage. He seemed to know we were working on it before we even got started."

"Yeah." I nod in agreement. "You make a good point."

Let him think GG's the mayor. Takes some heat off of me.

"Let's get down to the business at hand. We're going to play pickleball with the producer, so you need to look a little bit better than you did the other day. Up first, a lesson."

The ball machine is ready. After his little speech yesterday about all my privilege, I have no intention of making this easy on him.

"Jeans?"

"Your text wasn't clear. I didn't know what we were doing, so I came prepared for anything. And besides, this can't be that hard, Tip."

"Can you move around in those things?"

He lunges to the right and to the left, ending with a sumo squat.

"No problem here."

At least he has sneakers on. He takes off his hat and I cringe, seeing the white stripe again. He grabs something out of his pocket and puts it around his head. A sweatband.

"This isn't a joke. Just like those trivalve…"

"Bivalve," he corrects me.

"Whatever. Just like those are important to you, pickleball is important to me. Looking like an eighties aerobics instructor is not the look I'm going for."

"It'll keep the hair out of my eyes and distract from the paint you added to my 'do."

Since sweatbands aren't part of mainstream everyday style, he's going to need to stick to a hat when the producer's here.

I hand him a paddle, which he holds with his fingertips like a pencil.

"Cut it out!" We just played the other day. Albeit for ten minutes, but I know he knows how to hold a paddle. "Put your hand on the face of the paddle. Now slide your palm down and shake hands with the grip." He does as I say and I reach over and wrap his fingertips around the handle, leaving mine there for a second before I realize I'm touching Dave Sherman's fingers and they're stronger and warmer than I expected. I let go quickly, try to hide my shudder, and pick up my paddle. "Okay. Stand behind the baseline so you're ready to return the serve after it bounces on your side of the court." I position my feet and hinge at my hips. Dave stands and leans over like he's dead-lifting or about to touch his toes.

"Stand more erect, dude."

He doesn't, but he turns his head and looks right at me. "Erect?"

"Did you not understand me?"

"Been a long time since anyone's asked me to be erect."

He looks at me again and chuckles. And it hits me. Oops. I can feel my cheeks turning the same color as my hair.

"Stop acting like you're still in middle school," I say.

"I can just see the GG headline now. Tippy tells Dave to get erect on the court. Maybe we will have our own Netflix show, but on a different channel."

He's like Comedy Central over there.

"Enough. Can you be serious now?"

Dave gets back in position, standing up straight this time. I take the ball machine remote out of my pocket and hit start. The first ball comes and Dave hits it, nailing one of the hanging baskets my mom hung on the posts at the back of the court.

"Chill, dude. Bell will have your head if you wreck her flowers."

Why she put the baskets there to begin with is beyond me.

"Watch." I hit the next one and drop it inside the lines.

The next ball leaves the machine, and he tries it again, but this time he's got his arms all wrong. It's like he's in a batter's stance, ready for a pitch rather than waiting to return a serve.

"We're not swinging for the fences here. The ball must bounce on the serving side of the court before the other team can hit it after you return the serve. Hold your arms in front of you while you're waiting for the serve. Keep your paddle at hip level as you make contact with the ball." I hold my paddle out to the side and demonstrate.

He tries to imitate me, but he just can't get it right. I walk over and stand behind him, positioning his arms from behind. My hands barely fit around his forearms. They're soft with the tiniest bit of hair. The saltwater has done wonders for his skin. My chest rubs his back as I try to get a better grip on him, and I swear I hear him groan. I get him in the right position, but my body is betraying me as it leans into him. The next ball pops out of the machine. I let go of him and he swings to hit it, but I haven't moved back far enough and his elbow catches my eye, knocking me on my butt.

"Oh my gosh! Tippy!" He throws his paddle down and grabs both of my hands, prying them off my eye. "Shit. Let's get some ice."

It must look bad already. Dave places his hands on my arms and balances me as we stand up and walk toward my house.

"I'm sorry. Really. I didn't mean to do it." He keeps looking at my face. "Shit. Shit."

"It was an accident. Please chill out."

He puts his hand on my back to move me to the house a little faster. The bridge of my nose and my forehead are throbbing. Bear barks at Dave as we walk through the front door, but Dave ignores him.

I catch my reflection in the mirror and panic. It's red under my whole eye and turning purple. A black eye is the last thing I want for the TV producer's day on the island.

"DAVE!" I yell from the foyer.

I can hear the ice maker.

"Come here. Sit on your couch."

I make my way into the family room with Bear at my heels. Dave hands me a tea towel filled with ice and I glare at him with one good eye.

"What am I going to do now? Borrow one of Josh's pirate patches?"

Dave's brother used to perform as a pirate at kids' birthday parties. Ever since his stint as a professor, he's given it up, but I'm sure he still has an eye patch handy.

Dave's taken his sweatband off and looks like a skunk. Disaster! We're so far from camera ready!

I reach down and pull Bear up onto the couch with me. He nuzzles under my arm.

"When everyone asks what happened, what am I going to say? Dave elbowed me in the head? Raucous roll in the hay?"

I take the ice down for a second, and Dave pushes my hand back up.

"You can tell them the truth. It's kind of cute. You were giving me hands-on instruction for my pickleball stroke, and the rest is history."

"This," I point between us, "will never work!"

I slam the ice down on the couch. We've spent two days together and ended up with two visible changes to our bodies. When we go on an actual date, the casualties will be ridiculous. Apparently, we're combustible when we're together.

"Ice it, TFM."

"We are on two different wavelengths. We bicker back and forth. We misconstrue what the other person is saying. We're three cups taunting, a tablespoon of venom, and a sprinkle of salt. They'll see right through us when we're together."

He's sitting on my coffee table like a deer in headlights. Looking around, taking in my house. I'm worried I left something weird and embarrassing out but remember I have nothing weird and embarrassing.

He finally spits out, "Yeah, we are a potent chemical equation. That's for sure."

And I guess that's what they already felt on-screen during the meeting.

I sigh. "We have to balance it out in a positive way. Not creating World War III or causing permanent physical damage to either of us. Right now, it's not possible. I'm supposed to like you, and instead I want to cause you great bodily harm for giving me a black eye. They'll see right through me and know we aren't really dating."

Dave kneels down next to me on the floor. He looks at me and smiles. He has perfect teeth, and I can't remember if I've ever seen them this close up. He takes my arm, the one that's not holding the ice, and runs his thumb up and down my skin. The rough edge of his nail tickles the hairs on my arm. I swallow and despite myself, I tremble.

I pull my arm free and he says, "See? I made you shiver. I fooled even you into thinking I liked you. Imagine what we can make them see." He raises his eyebrows and blows me a kiss.

My limbs get heavy. I'm still as a statue. What is going on with me? I mean, I know I haven't dated anyone for a hot minute, but I shouldn't be catching chills from Dave this easily. Every part of my body is betraying me. Except my mind. I can keep that clear. And Dave is right. Unfortunately. They will believe it.

"Pull it together and keep your eye on the prize," he says, moving back to the coffee table.

"Game on, Sherman. Keep your head back and ice on."

I lean against the back of the couch. My eye throbs.

"Think you can grab some ibuprofen from the medicine cabinet without snooping through all of my stuff?"

Dave looks around, not knowing which way to go.

"Back room to the left."

"You know, if we were dating for real, you wouldn't keep any secrets from me." He walks toward my room.

"I don't have secrets. Just don't need you to know what tampons I use."

"Just another thing I'd know if we were dating," he yells from the bathroom. "Two or three?"

This seems like a job for as many as possible. "Three, please."

Dave brings me the pills with a glass of ice water.

"Thank you. You can go. I'll be fine."

He stands next to the couch, not moving. "I'm a little bit worried about the story you're going to spin about this. You know it won't benefit you to make me look bad."

"Are you threatening an injured woman?"

Dave puts his hat back on. "I wouldn't think of threatening any woman, injured or not. I just want to make sure the truth is always at the tip of your tongue."

"I'm not that nasty, Dave. Of course I'll tell the truth, albeit the way I remember it." I try to wink and realize I can't.

"Any false words and I'm out." And he walks to the door, taking our moments with him. "Later, Tip. I really am sorry."

My stomach feels the way it does right before I hit the top of a roller coaster. Scared. Nervous. And full of possibility. Most of it's because of *Love at the Last Resort*, but Dave's addition seems to have magnified all of my feelings about this. I could keep it in check before, but now my actions are anyone's guess. Spin my wheel and get Nausea for $100. Goosebumps for $50. Shivers for $500. I'm out of control, and if there's one thing I like, it's being one hundred percent in control of everything I do.

Bear jumps off the couch and runs to the door. I should have had Dave let him out while he was still here. I peer out the window and see Dave on the court, picking up all our balls. I try to smile but my cheeks hurt. Bear's whining at the door, but I'm not letting him out while Dave's still here. So I stand and watch until he goes. But before he gets in the truck, he looks at the house and right into the window. And points to himself, then his eyes, and then to me. *I see you.* I die a thousand deaths and vow to avoid windows anytime Dave's around.

He pulls out of the driveway, and I text Sylviane while I sit on the front steps and Bear takes care of his business.

Tippy: How much concealer do you have at the ready?

Sylviane: Why on earth are you looking for concealer?

Tippy: Dave and I played pickleball.

Sylviane: I don't want to know, but I've got you covered (literally). Will bring it over later.

GREENSEA GAZETTE

Islanders,

We can confirm that was the new weekly ferry ballet performance you saw taking place in the middle of Grays Bay. It's a grand idea, meant for smaller boats, but they sure got the water churning rhythmically. Might we suggest the high school sailing team take over the water vessel ballet? Their sailboats might be more appropriately sized, and who wouldn't love synchronized sailing?

An investigation has been opened by the folks at Wine Down to figure out how Mr. Guserevel knew all the correct answers to the trivia questions last night. Knowing that a fifteen-horned dinosaur existed and was called a Kosmoceratops proved to be the straw that broke the camel's back. Who knows that? And why?

XOXO,

GG

DAVE

I pull up at my cousin's place, The Old Owl, just as Tippy's getting out of her car. She's taking this date seriously. Dressed in tight dark blue jeans, tall brown boots, and a lacy white top. Her long red hair hangs down her back in perfect curls. My flannel and jeans suddenly feel a little underdressed.

I try to get a closer look at her eye as I walk toward her. From this distance, she looks healed.

"Hey," Tippy says across the parking lot.

I cock my head to each side, trying to get a better look.

"You can just ask how it is, you know." She pulls her hair off her face. From about two feet away I can see the outline of a bruise under her eye, but it's not that bad.

"Wow! I didn't do that much damage!"

"Dude, I have clown makeup on trying to hide it. Trust me, you did enough damage."

I keep my hat on. Don't want to show her my new look from Greensea Glam right away.

"We're going to do our own recording today. Just pretend

like we're making videos along the way. I spoke to Quinn, so she sort of knows what we're doing." Tippy says.

Oh great. Quinn's in on this too. Just a matter of time before everyone knows. "Sort of?"

"Yeah. I told her it was for the paper. Kind of a tourism thing. She knows nothing about the show."

"But she thinks we're on a date together?"

"Yep. I told her we were doing a feature on the oysters so you agreed to help me with this. It's not a complete lie."

I mentally plan all the texts I'm going to send to my friends and family after people hear about this crap. I'll never hear the end of it.

"Let's get this fake date over with." I hold the solid all-wood door open for Tippy.

This place is like my second home. I love it here. Windows offer sweeping views of the bay. Fishing nets drape across the ceiling, and buoys from crab pots hang on the shiplap walls. The musty smell of saltwater mixes with the grease from fries. What more could you want?

Quinn puts us at a table in the corner with no one near us at the moment. It's pretty quiet on a Tuesday night. I imagine that's why Tippy picked it. We sit down and I take off my hat.

"Dave Sherman!" Tippy squeals. Surprise reveal worked just as I planned.

I do one of my head flips out of habit, but there's nothing there to move. Tippy's going to have to pick her jaw up from the table.

"You got rid of the paint!" Tippy stands up and looks at my profile. "Not bad." She nods her head and sits back down. "I told you Glenda could fix you up."

Quinn walks up to take our order. "What can I get ya? Whoa! Dude! Where's your hair?"

"Had an unfortunate run-in with a paintbrush." I glance at Tippy.

Quinn looks at both of us and shrugs. "The usual for each of you?"

"Yep, cranberry vodka for me," says Tippy.

"Whatever IPA you have on draft this week, Q," I say.

Quinn and I are cousins. She's older, and her family moved away during her pivotal growing-up years. We've made up for lost time though. Bonded over oysters and food service. She and her partner, Amanda, are the best front-porch visitors. They sit for hours and talk about restoring their old house, right in Grays Bay, close to The Old Owl. Typical Cape Cod style you'd find along many coasts, but they've restored it using one hundred percent local supplies. Wood, nails, paint—you name it, it comes from this area. I love talking to them about it. They're so proud of every inch, and the love and care they're taking shows. It's kind of like how I am with my oysters. And I've got nothing but respect for it.

"So are we ordering food, Tip?" I'm not sure what the exact plan is. I figure we could technically film this whole thing in about three minutes and get out of here, but it looks like we're settling in.

"This is a date. What'd you think it was, slam, bam, thank you ma'am?" Tippy quips. She puts her hair behind her ears and raises her eyebrows.

"So we're ordering food." I peruse the menu even though I have it all memorized.

"Yes, and get something that won't get stuck in your teeth. We don't need a piece of kale hanging out in your mouth in our video." She looks down at the menu and moves her fingers across items crossing them off, presumably the ones with dental hazards.

"I never order kale when I'm here. No need to worry."

Quinn brings over our drinks and sets them on the table.

"Can I get you some food, or do you need a minute?"

"Can't resist your club, cuz."

Quinn rolls her eyes. "Maybe someday you'll branch out. You know, we have a full menu here, even though you and your siblings get the same thing every time."

Habits are hard to break.

"What's the best item on your menu?" asks Tippy.

Quinn thinks about it and, with her eyes staring down at the floor, says, "The club."

I slam my hands on the table. "Need I say more!"

"Well, I guess I'll give it a go," Tippy answers.

"See? Tippy's branching out. You're usually a Cobb Salad hold the bacon customer."

"Who eats the Cobb without bacon?" I ask and Tippy tuts me and rolls her eyes.

"I'll leave you two to your date." Quinn snickers and heads back to the kitchen.

The words Tippy and date give me indigestion even on an empty stomach. Tippy grabs her phone and turns it to selfie mode.

"Hi. Dave and I," she points it toward me, "are at Greensea's best pub, The Old Owl!"

She takes a quick video of the bar around us, getting a shot of the owl above the bar, and then stops filming.

"How 'bout you tell the origin of The Old Owl, since it's your family's story?"

"On camera?" I ask.

"Of course!"

I guess it's easier than most of the things she could ask me to do, so I agree. She sets up the camera pointed right at me.

"This place used to be my Grandpa's, and now it belongs to my cousin, Quinn. Legend has it this owl," I point above the bar and Tippy follows with her phone, "lived in the tree outside the bar for many years, calling to my grandfather every night as he walked to his truck. One night my grandpa found him lying in the bed of his truck. Dead. Natural causes. Like he was asking to be saved for posterity. He changed the name from Sherman's Pub to The Old Owl in its honor."

Tippy stops filming.

"See? That was easy! A little Greensea color."

That wasn't bad. I love sharing my family history. This island's filled with it too.

"You done filming us?"

"We'll play darts after dinner so I can get some more footage. I bet Quinn will video it for us, since it's not too crowded."

Should've guessed we weren't done.

"I'm going to take you down, Meadowcroft." I point at her for emphasis.

"Nice, Dave. Remember we're on a date? Try to summon a little bit of the compassion you had after you knocked me down on the court."

Tippy plus me does not equal compassion unless of course she's injured and I don't intend to injure her with the darts. Although...

The server brings our club sandwiches. I take a bigger than normal bite and I'm conscious of every move my mouth makes, worried I might have mayo dripping down my face or ham stuck in my teeth. Eating across from Tippy is the scariest first date I've ever been on.

"How are your mom and dad?" I ask, trying to make conversation to shake my nerves.

"Oh, you know. They're amazing. Just running the newspaper and the shop. How about your parents? Are they still enjoying being on the island?"

My parents took an extended vacation to Europe last summer, thanks to an exorbitant and gracious fee Johnny Nickel paid them to rent their house.

"Nah. They're chomping at the bit to get out of here again."

Tippy takes a bite of her sandwich. She eats it daintily with her pinky up. She picks up her napkin and dots around her mouth after each bite. "Back to Europe?"

"Nope. They're waiting for their RV to be delivered. Going to travel the United States."

I'm still in shock that that's their plan. I don't think they'll be able to stick to it, but they say they're selling the house and going on the road. Josh, Jac, Ollie, and I keep appeasing them and saying it's all great, but deep down, none of us wants them to sell the house we grew up in, and no one thinks Mom will spend that much time with Dad in a tin can.

"Wow," says Tippy. "That seems out of character."

That may be the only thing Tippy and I agree on.

I finish my beer, and Quinn brings me another and a different drink for Tippy this time.

"What's that?" I ask.

"I'm a one drink girl. This is cranberry tonic. Quinn knows I never have more than one. Even when you trick some random bar patron into buying me a drink, she only brings me this."

Sounds like Quinn. Always looking out for her customers. But I'll have to have a word with her, because I'm certain she's charged me for actual cocktails when I've tried to do that to Tippy.

"Darts?"

We stand up and walk over to the dartboard. There's only one other table filled with people in the corner, and I've never seen them. Probably tourists looking for a restaurant and found The Old Owl because it's the only thing open on a Tuesday.

Tippy walks up to the bar and hands Quinn her phone.

"Mind getting some footage of me taking him down?" she asks Quinn.

"Be happy to. Sorry, cuz," says Quinn.

Tippy grabs the darts and walks back to the line.

"Age before beauty," she says, and hands them to me.

I loosen up my shoulders. Adjust my stance. But just as I'm about to shoot, she yells, "Wait!" I turn toward her as her fingers reach toward my face.

"Random crumb of bread," she says, and brushes something off my chin. My entire body tingles when her hand touches me. Something in me short circuits at the gentle touch of the tip of her finger, and I can hardly turn toward the dartboard. I have to heel toe my feet and twist my body to make the rest of me go in that direction. I will my arm to raise into position and I throw a dart, miss the board, and hit the kitchen door.

"What the hell, Dave?" yells Quinn behind the phone.

I eek out, "Sorry."

I blink twice, worried I might be having a stroke. What was that? And what's wrong with me? I go to the door and remove the dart. Thankfully it's only a tiny hole; at least I didn't hit the window and there wasn't anyone coming out of the kitchen at the same time.

"Why's the dartboard so close to the kitchen door?" I can't be the only person who's hit it before.

"It's not that close! Unless your arm points to the door, you won't come close to it. In my ten years owning this place, that has never, ever happened. That was a terrible throw." Quinn's reached the point of exasperation but gets ready to film again.

Tippy sighs and I give the next one a go. At least I hit the board this time, and the next. The momentary electrical problem in my whole body's over and not going to happen again.

I walk up and remove the darts. "Sorry about that. You just made me nervous when you went for my face," I say to Tippy.

"Yeah, wiping a crumb off your chin is the same as wielding a butcher's knife at your heart," Tippy says.

"That's what it felt like you were about to do," I say, lying because it wasn't fear I felt. Something stirred in me, and I kind of wished I had a hundred more crumbs on my chin.

Tippy takes the darts. She positions her feet at the line and pulls one arm back. Her lacy blouse flows with her figure. She launches the first dart right into a bullseye. She looks right at Quinn to make sure she was recording it.

"Get that?" she asks.

"Sure did!" Quinn answers.

"Really?" I ask. Never figured Tippy Meadowcroft for an ace dart player.

"Really," Tippy answers.

Her next two shots aren't quite bullseyes, but they're close, and that's the only thing that counts in darts. I'd better step it up, or I'm going to lose to Tippy Freaking Meadowcroft and I will never hear the end of it.

I keep them on the dartboard during my next turn but can't manage a bullseye. We go back and forth until Tippy has a round of three bullseyes and I wonder if she's using magnets or Velcro.

"Are you trying out for the Olympics?" I didn't know I was playing against a professional.

"I had to get good. We have a dartboard at the house, and I willed myself to be better than Simon. I could beat you with my eyes closed."

"Yeah, I played my brothers too, but most of the time it was a game of dares and not real darts." Mom made us stop after Oliver had to go to the island urgent care with a dart stuck in his butt.

Maybe this is what has always scared me about Tippy. The precision with which she moves around. Every move executed to make sure she wins, or at the very least, succeeds. It's something I could never compete with, so I resorted to sabotage.

"You two done here?" Quinn asks.

I look around and we're the only two left.

Tippy gives Quinn her credit card. "A business expense."

And we walk out to the parking lot. I walk her to her car and open the door, sticking my hand out for a handshake.

"Is this how you end all your dates?"

"Only the ones that are a business arrangement!"

Tippy opens her arms. I follow. And we hug, like robots, our bodies as stiff as boards. I fight the urge to wrap her in my arms. I pat her back like she's been an obedient dog, go to my car, and throw my head back on the headrest.

CHAPTER THIRTEEN

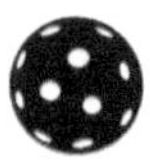

TIPPY

Before Dave and I went on our date, I got some footage of The Old Owl. I walked up to the front to get the quaint old pub feel. Walked through the doors and onto the back deck, getting a magnificent view of the harbor and an incoming ferry. I wanted the beginning to have all the vibes. Because as soon as Dave and I were the focus, I knew it would be awkward. And I was right. The bit at the table looks staged, probably because it is. And the darts game has all of our old school banter front and center. I just have to hope whatever they saw during our meeting, they see again in this piece. I cut and clip the video. Add in the part of me wiping Dave's chin to make it a little more intimate. I watch the video over and over, hoping I'll see something they'll like. It's funny and cute, and I hope it has enough energy for them.

My phone pings with an alert from the paper forcing me to stop watching the video for the seventeenth time.

Rumor has it a reality show everyone loves to hate may be coming to Greensea.

What in the actual hell! Shit. Shit. Shit. How did someone other than me post to GG's account? I went straight to bed last night and didn't write a column. Who took it upon themselves to do my dirty work? I call my dad and he doesn't pick up. I use our 911 signal, a quick one ring and then a call back, so he'll know it's serious.

"Good gosh, Tip. What's up?" he says as soon as he answers. "I'm in a meeting with the accountant."

"Someone posted to the GG account. Who's in the office?"

"Just the new intern, Tabby."

"Give me her number."

"Calm down, darling. I'll have her call you."

I hang up. How'd she do this? Is there an insecure computer in the building?

I answer before the first ring's done.

"Did you just post an alert for GG?"

"Yes!" says a voice who sounds like she's about to be congratulated.

"Why'd you do that?"

"Oh, well, someone called, and I thought I'd send out the blast for GG. The column's anonymous, so I didn't know who to call. Your dad's been in meetings, so I figured it would be helpful."

I have so many questions.

"It wasn't. Do not under any circumstances do anything like that again or you will lose your job."

"I'm sorry." She sniffs. Great. Probably made the girl cry. But I don't even care. There's only one GG in this town, and that's me.

"How'd you know how to send a blast for GG?" I thought I was the only one who had that ability.

"If you look, I didn't send it from GG, I just sent it to our general subscribers."

Even more people than if she'd narrowed it down to just the GG subscribers. Although there aren't many islanders who don't subscribe to GG.

No choice but to move into damage control now. "Who called? Did they give a name? What did their voice sound like?"

"Well, it was a woman. She didn't leave her name, obviously. But she said she heard it from a very reliable source."

"Thanks," I say and hang up, wishing I had an actual receiver to slam down and not an unsatisfying button on a screen to push.

I think back. Sylviane and Dave are the only people who know. Sylviane would not have told a soul. It has to be that damn Dave.

I call Dave. He doesn't answer. I try a 911 ring on him. Nothing. So I text him.

> Tippy: Why did you spill the beans on this little project?

I stare at my phone, waiting for the three dots to appear. Still not a thing. So I text again.

> Tippy: Was this to get me back for the paint in your hair? I knew you weren't to be trusted. It's just like that time you found out I got a B in AP Earth Science and blabbed it to the whole school. Nothing is sacred with you. NO WONDER YOU HANG OUT WITH SHELLS ALL DAY AND YOU'RE STILL SINGLE.

All caps for emphasis. I'm so mad. I get out my all-purpose

spray and a rag and start cleaning every inch of the counter. Spray. Wipe furiously. Spray again. The soft smell of lavender fills the kitchen but doesn't calm my nerves.

Why would he tell anyone? I can't believe he's done this after all I did for Sherman's Shellfish.

I retrace my steps for the last few days to think of everywhere I've been. Anything I've seen that would point to someone leaking this. I've had no one, other than Dave, at the house. Mom and Dad don't even know.

Sylviane's as tight-lipped as they come. Mostly because she doesn't know anyone. When we were getting our nails done, she…And then I realize it's my fault. I told her at the nail spa. Of course, Ann, or one of her workers, must have heard us and made the tip. My own flipping fault. Figures. No more mistakes. I have to button this up.

I grab my phone and try to erase the text I sent to Dave. I know there's a way to do that on this newfangled thing. I highlight it but it's not one of the choices. Shit.

This is one of those moments it would have paid off to take a second and breathe before I sent an angry message. In my defense, it was too important.

So I send another…

Tippy: Oops! Sorry! Wasn't you.

Casual. Breezy. Like I haven't said anything at all.

As soon as I send it, Dad calls.

"Well, honey, I just got a call from Mayor Nickerbottom. Tell me what you know about the anonymous tip that's got you in a little tizzy."

This isn't how I wanted to tell them about what I'm trying to do, but I don't have a choice thanks to Tabby, the intern.

Deep breath in. One. Two. Three...And I explain it to him leaving out the Dave part.

"Okay. Okay. Well, Mayor Nickerbottom's called a town meeting for tonight, so get your ducks in a row."

I flop down on my couch. I cover my face with a pillow, forgetting about my eye. Ouch! Great. Now I have to go lay out my case in front of the whole town and make them think Dave and I are in love. Not at all what I feel like doing. Islanders come out of the woodwork for town meetings. Tonight will be no exception.

Operation-Calm-Myself-and-Make-Myself-as-Presentable-as-Possible-for-Tonight. First step, cold shower to calm down my nervous system and make me feel a little more sane.

I text Dave again.

> Tippy: Let's drive to the town meeting together. Meet me here at 5:30 and we'll review the plan.
>
> Dave: What meeting?
>
> Tippy: Well...it seems Nickerbottom's got his knickers up his bottom. He's called a town meeting for tonight to discuss Love at the Last Resort coming to the island. We can review the plan beforehand.
>
> Dave: No way.
>
> Tippy: But we agreed!
>
> Dave: You're a little too mean and bossy, Tippy.
>
> Tippy: I'm sorry. I panicked. Please come to the meeting.
>
> Dave: We'll see.

He has to come. Whether or not I want to believe it, Dave

lends credibility to this project. It's less a random thing Tippy wants to do and more a merging of two upstanding Greensea families.

The cold water clears my head, and I'm ready to move ahead with my emergency plan.

GREENSEA GAZETTE

Islanders,

We did not know our anonymous tip line would be such a success and bring immediate satisfaction! Kudos and thank you! Keep the tips coming!

GG has done some digging, and we can report with great confidence that our own Tippy Meadowcroft is in talks to bring Love at the Last Resort *to our fair isle. Imagine that, a network TV show featuring Greensea. We've hit the jackpot! And even better, there's an unsubstantiated rumor that she's teamed up with Dave Sherman to make this happen. Our ears will be open at the town meeting tonight. We'll be waiting with bated breath to see why these two think this is a good idea!*

XOXO,

GG

CHAPTER FOURTEEN

TIPPY

The town meeting is in the all-denominational island church. It seems odd to mix church and state, but it works on Greensea, where everything's a little mixed up. Tonight, it's standing room only because everyone wants to hear what I'm up to with *Love at the Last Resort*. I look around. My whole Pilates crew is here. All my teachers from grade school. The Fit Greenies. Pretty much every shop owner. This place is packed with people.

Dave refused to drive with me, but at least he did the right thing and showed up at the church. We're smack dab in the front pew with Josh and Sylviane reluctantly beside us.

"Let's call this meeting to order," says the mayor, banging the gavel on some books. "Our first and only matter is Tippy Meadowcroft's unlawful entry of Greensea into the contest to be on that ridiculous TV show."

"Mayor, I believe you're supposed to be impartial," says Josh in a deadpan voice. I turn, look at him, and give him my most gracious smile.

"I don't think anyone on this island is impartial where this is concerned," Mayor Nickerbottom responds.

"Josh is right," I chime in. "You're supposed to be a mediator. You facilitate the conversation with an unbiased opinion."

The mayor rolls his eyes. "Alright, Tippy. Explain your proposal."

He sits back in his chair, arms crossed on his chest, and with a look that reads, "I've already made up my mind."

"Thank you, Mayor." I stand up, ignore him, and turn toward the rows of islanders who've gathered to voice their opinions. "And thank you all for coming." I run my hands down my pencil skirt as I take a strategic pause. Silence is key in any presentation.

"Not long ago, our fair Greensea was portrayed on TV as the island of a scorned woman, our one and only Jac. We took sides. Had Team Jac signs up all over. Even though Jac, and by extension, our island, was maligned, we all came together rallying around a cause. We need that kind of spirit on the island again. It's our time to show the world that we are so much more than that. Let them see the beauty of our shores. The quaint nature of our town. The charming faces of our residents."

"But Johnny Nickel showed them that with his hit single," yells someone in the back.

Of course someone would bring that up. "Johnny only showed us his love for Jac. He didn't show the world what a perfect place this is to live, visit, enjoy."

"Why do we want to tell anyone that?" asks Jessica Read. "There'll just be more tourists if we do that."

"More tourists are not a bad thing," I answer.

"Says you," comments Josh. I glare at him, hoping I'll burn a hole in his pants with my eyes.

"Tourists boost our economy. They help people make ends meet," I offer.

"And they make it harder to get around," croaks a voice in the third or fourth pew. "How would it work with a film crew? That's going to cause backups all over the island. Our roads aren't built to handle that much traffic."

"The film crew would be concentrated around Swifterson. When they travel to other sites, they will work with a skeleton crew. No inconvenience to any of us."

"Will the eligible bachelors be available to date?" asks a giggly college-aged girl in the back.

"Will islanders be contestants?" asks a divorcee in the front.

"We hope they will use islanders and people they've identified as contestants. It's important to put our best foot forward so they can see the benefits of filming on Greensea," I answer. "Dave and I have shown them as much as we can. Now it's our turn to do this together." I motion to the crowd like I'm serving a platter.

"Back up a bit. How in this green island's name are you and Dave Sherman working together?" Mayor Nickerbottom questions.

"We're dating," I say in my softest and sweetest voice, giving my eyelashes a little flutter.

A snicker crosses the room.

"Just because GG hasn't reported it doesn't mean it can't be true!" My voice reaches a higher pitch.

Dave is crossing his legs and uncrossing them next to me.

"You're telling me you two have gone from mortal enemies to a cuddly couple, and somehow none of us noticed?" The mayor acts as the sound piece for the island.

I nod my head and smile. "Mayor, you saw us working together on Sherman's Shellfish the other day."

The mayor squints his eyes. "How do we know you don't have a little quid pro quo going? I mean, the centerpieces that have shown up at Sherman's have Bell's name all over them."

He's right. They do. Oyster shells with hand-painted gold rims around them. I made them, but got the idea from Mom.

"Be honest, Tippy! You and Dave aren't even real!" Mayor Nickerbottom gives me a stern look.

The little hairs on the back of my neck are standing up. I can feel all the eyes watching me like I'm the panda about to give birth at the zoo. I've got to do something. And quickly. To seal the deal. To prove them all wrong. I grab Dave's hand and pull him up so he's standing next to me.

"What do you mean, it's not real?" I raise both of our hands like I'm holding a trophy to prove my worth. "We're moving in together!"

I squeeze Dave's hand a little harder, threatening him not to say a word. Mayor Nickerbottom leans his head to the left. "Now, Tippy, we all know that's not true."

"It is! Dave's moving his things into Meadowcroft this weekend."

I feel Dave's nails dig into my palms. There's a hum that takes over the church. I look at Dave with my best googly eyes. And in return he looks at me like I've eaten his last oyster.

Our relationship just went from zero to sixty. Oops. A deep breath or anything would have been better than opening my mouth. It's been well established that thinking before I speak is not my strong suit, and now I don't have time to think about what I've done. Again. Why aren't I chewing gum?

"How'd you get that black eye, Tippy?" asks someone in the back.

"That's none of your business," I grunt toward the back of the room.

"Dave, what happened to your hair?" questions another meeting attendee.

The mayor looks to me and looks to Dave, who's holding his head in his hand.

"I don't want to know what kind of things are going on behind closed doors with the two of you, but I think we're ready to take a vote on this charade," says the mayor.

"Wait. Does anyone have any other questions?" I plead. He has to give them time to ask before they vote.

"Are you getting paid for this, Tippy?" my sixth grade science teacher, Mr. Crenshaw, asks.

"No. But the revenue we bring in will most definitely help the paper. So to be honest, I will receive some compensation indirectly. And think about what this could mean for our entire island. We will highlight all the island treasures. People will want to visit and spend money."

"It'll raise our home values," says Nora Cunningham, one of the island's highest performing realtors.

"And our taxes," says the mayor.

"Maybe the city can use the money to create covered pickle-ball courts at Sunset Tower Park. Or a new swimming pool. Or to fix up the ferry. With an influx of money, more things are possible on Greensea." I'm pulling things out of my butt. Trying to find something that will tug at their heartstrings.

"All in favor?" asks the mayor, not bothering to see if there are any more questions.

A bunch of people raise their hands. They all look at each other, and more raise their hands when they see their neighbors saying yes. It's like a case of chicken pox running through a classroom. Everyone's saying yes. My smile grows wider than I thought possible. Mayor Nickerbottom's assistant is busy counting all the hands in the air.

"All opposed?"

Three people raise their hands. Mayor Nickerbottom, his assistant, and Old Man Jackson.

The mayor shakes his head. "I think we need a revote. People aren't thinking properly."

Josh speaks up. "That's not right. Tippy won fair and square."

"Will someone please explain to me why you all voted for this monstrosity?" asks the mayor.

Laura Prescott stands up.

"I don't know why everyone did, but I think we all like the excitement that's buzzing around. Living on an island can be boring and isolating. Even mundane. This brings a little bit of the big city into our lives for a short time."

Great answer. I'll thank her at Pilates tomorrow—even if she's stolen my reformer once again.

"And we like to work together," offers Mr. Crenshaw.

"And I, for one, just want to see the romance between Dave and Tippy blossom," says Quinn.

Mental note—never go to The Old Owl again.

"Well, what do you need from us?" asks the mayor, resigned that this is happening.

"I need everyone to do what they can to clean up their area. Get out your spring flowers. Freshen up the chipped paint on your front porch. Put your best foot forward in any way you can."

"Might want to invest in some concealer for yourself. That shiner on your eye sure won't look good on TV," says the mayor as he hits his gavel on the books to end the meeting.

———

After the meeting, Dave heads straight for the grotto next to the church parking lot. I follow so close that I heel one of his shoes. He turns around, almost spitting his words. "I am not moving into your place."

"But Dave..." is all I can get out before he's talking again.

"First, we're not together. Did you forget that this is all a ruse for your little plan?" he whisper-shouts at me.

"I know we're not, and you know we're not, but everyone else thinks we are."

The breeze off the Sound is blowing the grotto's candle flames, which I can't take my eyes off of as I send silent wishes toward them, hoping that Dave will actually fall in line with what I just proposed.

"Second, you know there's no way I can leave the oysters alone like that."

People are making their way out of the church, so I walk Dave deeper into the grotto so we can't be seen, or heard, from the parking lot. Wait a minute, a "second" comment implies there isn't a closed door. Reasoning with him may prevail.

"Well, what do you expect? Me to move into your cottage?" The idea's preposterous, but if he'll only accept it that way, then I'll do it.

"How about no one moves anywhere! This was not part of the deal. You've been watching too many rom-coms. This is real life. People don't just move in with each other because of some half-baked scheme."

Things escalated, but what else was I supposed to say? Mom always says apologies get you further, so I look up at Dave with my softest eyes and say, "I'm sorry. I only ever meant to help the island, the oyster farm, the newspaper..."

I look down at the gravel path and wait for him to reply. He takes a deep breath, and I'm pretty sure I calmed him down.

"Look, I know this thing means a lot to you, and you've done quite a bit of work on the oyster farm in return for my companionship. But it has to end now."

My gentle demeanor falls to the side. Not a chance in hell. We've come this far, and Tippy Meadowcroft has never given up.

"Think back, Dave." I hold his eyes with mine. "You started this with your little antics. You left me without a choice."

"One option would have been to just keep your mouth shut."

I grab his arm. He stops and looks at me. My eyes tear, not because I'm upset but because of the amount of makeup I'm wearing. He tenses his forearm, and I feel all the muscles beneath his flannel go rigid. His free hand reaches up to my face and wipes away one of my tears. He shakes his head and his arm free and walks toward his truck. I try to follow as close as I can.

Meredith from the gem store catches up to us. Probably has some woo-woo crap to tell us about the moon or some sage to sell us that will clear our energy.

"Tippy, Dave, I'm not sure what you've got going on here." We both turn and look at her as she raises both hands in a circular motion. "But the aura the two of you have around you when you're near each other is red."

"What's that supposed to mean, Mer? Impending epic bloodshed battle?" asks Dave.

"No. There's a ton of pent-up passion between you two. Can't believe I never noticed it before. Come to think of it, I've just never seen you standing next to each other like this."

She walks past us and turns around. "At least you know the universe is on your side with this," she makes quotes with her fingers, "relationship."

Dave gets to his truck and mumbles, "No dice, Tip. I'll keep up the dating charade, but I'm not moving in."

Quick. Think. How can I make him see this is a good idea? What else does he want? Dave pulls out of the parking lot and I wander over to my car.

"Lover's quarrel?" asks Josh.

"No. He's just going home to pack."

"Sure he is."

Sylviane slugs his arm and they head toward their car.

Bell and Topper walk over to me. "Sweetie," says Bell. "I had no idea you two were an item. How could we live so close to each other and not know something so important?" Bell's eyes tear up.

"Mom? Can we go home and talk?"

She wraps me in a hug and Topper says, "I'll put the kettle on."

Chamomile tea and honey's been the one thing that's helped me relax since I was a teenager. That and one of Mom's snickerdoodles. Perfect balm for my soul.

I drive home, park in my driveway, and walk over to Mom and Dad's. A linen-scented candle burns on the counter. The lights are dim; Mom always prefers lamps to set the mood.

"What's going on, sweetheart?"

I pick up the sky blue teacup decorated with little roses and take a sip of the warm liquid.

"I didn't mean for any of this to happen..." I tell them my idea for *Love at the Last Resort* and the unfortunate coincidence that led me to telling the producers that Dave and I are together.

"Oh dear," says Topper. "I feel a little responsible."

"What do you mean?" I ask.

"I'm the one who sent Dave over to install the lights. If I hadn't done that, none of this would have happened."

"Don't go blaming yourself, Topper. You meant nothing by that," says Bell. She looks at me. Her eyes are soft in the dim light. "Do you have any feelings for Dave?"

Feelings for Dave Sherman? Yeah. I have feelings, but they're not of the take-me-to-bed kind. Whatever's going on inside of me is way different than that.

I must have a guilty look on my face, because my mom looks

at me and says, "Remember, there are many reasons people get together. It's not always for love at first."

I'm quiet for the first time in a long time. Normally I would have launched into a thousand things that are wrong with Dave, and now the first thing I'm thinking about are his strong forearms that shuck oysters instead of how I can torture him.

"That doesn't matter. This is all an act. What do I do now?"

"Maybe it's time you started telling the truth," says Dad.

But before I have to answer, my phone pings with a text from Dave.

It's a grocery list.

> Dave: Sweet Cream – Coffee – Blueberry Danish

And then another:

> Dave: The least you can do is stock your fridge with all the things I need in the morning.

My cheeks flush, and I feel an actual tear in my eye. I can't help but smile. What on earth convinced him this was something he should do?

"What was that?" asks Mom.

"A morning grocery list from Dave."

Bell and Topper exchange a look.

"What?" I ask.

"Nothing," says Topper. "Just had a feeling this mortal enemy act would change sometime, and you'd realize you two had an unbelievable chemistry."

Mom chimes in. "We saw it long ago when you were both up on stage performing during your third grade play about states. It was like you had sparks coming off the two of you. Always knew if you had the chance, the sparks would turn into quite a relationship."

Sparks? Us? My parents have been thinking, hoping, we'd get together since we were in elementary school? When I got lunch detention for taping him inside a box, somehow they saw love instead of hate. Weird. Between Meredith's words and theirs, I just hope the producers see what everyone else does.

"I'd better go. Need to make up the bed in the guest room."

CHAPTER FIFTEEN

DAVE

Damn tears. Box-turtle-in-distress routine makes me do crazy things. I packed a backpack and went over to Tippy's last night. The main thing that makes this arrangement difficult is needing to get up early and head to the bay. I can't roll out of bed and throw my waders on. Instead, it's get up and drive. At least the bed was literally the best thing I've ever slept in. I'm not sure what Egyptian cotton is, but I feel like I've been wrapped up like a mummy overnight. Leave it to Tippy to have the best. The bathroom is filled with soaps and lotions that have the scent of a fresh herb garden after a morning rain, without being girly or feminine. I swear I didn't read that off the side of the package, but it's the first thing that came to mind when the scent wafted up to my nose as I washed my hands.

It's hard to see in the kitchen because it's so early and the only light's coming from a little lamp in the corner of the counter. The last time I was in here I was rushing around trying to get her ice after I accidentally decked her. I didn't have time to take it all in. This place isn't half bad. I love the mix of butcher block counters, green cabinets, and stainless steel modern appliances. The stove stands out. It's a gigantic, old Italian stove. Not modern like the rest, instead calling attention to itself, stealing the show. Kind of like Tippy.

She's got some newfangled press for her coffee. I saw one of these at Jac's place in San Francisco, and I don't know how to work it. I'll bring my old-fashioned Mr. Coffee over later.

There's a blueberry Danish on the counter next to the sink. Wow. She listened. That must mean she went to Island Grocers after I sent my text last night, because there's no way Tippy eats this over-processed delight. I rip open the box and tear off a piece of Danish. Just like I'm at home.

As it melts in my mouth, a bark startles me, and I drop the piece to the ground. The little yip scared the crap out of me. My heart's racing, and Bear just ran off with my breakfast. I look up and see Tippy standing with her hands on her hips.

"Dave!" A couple of decibels too loud for this early.

"Shit, Tippy. That little thing scared me! And a quieter greeting would suffice."

"What do you expect? It's four thirty in the morning!"

"And? I have to get over to the bay. I like to be out there at five."

"What the hell?"

A cream silk or satin, who can tell the difference, eye mask holds her red curls out of her face. Her pajamas are the same cream button-down top and short shorts. I look away. It's not right to see your archenemy in clothes like this.

"What do you mean, what the hell? I told you this would be hard because I have to get up and work."

"Could you have at least been a little quiet?"

Quiet? I've been tiptoeing around this place. Didn't bang a single thing. "Your ears super powered or something? I'm like a little church mouse!"

I tear off another piece of the Danish. "That dog of yours is eating my breakfast."

She walks over and picks Bear up. He's a pile of brown curls in her arms. "Bear would only take something from you if you offered it to him."

I look at him nuzzling into her so innocently. But then he turns to me and gives me a little growl.

"Real ferocious." I roll my eyes.

"You're going to have to put off getting to the shells until five. I need at least seven hours of sleep."

"Maybe you should go to bed earlier, because I can't deviate."

I haven't had any coffee yet, and I can feel my blood boiling over. This was her idea. I am not agreeing to her schedule. She's going to have to bend a little to make this work. Not me!

"Stop." Tippy takes the eye mask off her head and sets it on her butcher block island. "I can hear the words moving around in your head and I don't want to hear it again. You're doing me a favor. I get it. Here you go, Dave, in or out. It's your last chance to take off and let me do this on my own. If you stay, I don't want to hear another word about how you're helping me out."

I take the rest of the Danish and head for the door, only turning around to say, "I'll bring my coffee pot over later. That thing sucks."

I can practically hear Tippy marking down the point she just won on her imaginary scoreboard. Then I kick myself for not being able to say no to someone who's been my rival since the beginning.

It's quiet and dark as I pull out of Meadowcroft. I see Kyler's milk truck pulling down the lane. Yes, Greensea still has a milkman who delivers fresh milk once a week. That's probably why people panicked last week when Kyler's cows were loose and running around the south end of the island.

Just imagine having to buy regular old milk from Island Grocers. What a travesty that would be! It took three high school kids to put their cars in strategic positions to cordon the cows until Kyler got there with some rope and walked them home.

Dad's sitting on my porch when I pull up.

"Were you going to tell us you moved out?"

My dad's an early riser, just like me. He gets up at the crack of dawn to get the paper and bring Mom a coffee. It's a tradition he's had for as long as I can remember.

"I didn't move out." I shut the truck door.

"That's not what I heard."

Great. The Greensea rumor mill's been working in overdrive.

"Mom got a call from the captain of the Fit Greenies last night. They're all in a tizzy about the town meeting."

"Surprised you weren't there."

"Ah, you know. We're not into that stuff anymore. Mom and I have one foot off the island. No need for us to go to those meetings these days."

Dad leans back in the porch chair and folds his arms across his body.

"So you and Tippy Meadowcroft? Mom says she knew the moment she got a note from Ms. Frankel about you teasing her in third grade."

I roll my eyes. "It's for the show."

Dad shakes his head and chews on a piece of grass, the weirdest habit he's had for as long as I can remember. This whole fake-living-together situation is going to be more trouble than it's worth, but maybe after everyone knows, things will calm down and we can just go about our business.

"So are you living over there? What's going on?"

"I stayed in Tippy's guest room last night. One thing lead to another at the town meeting, and she felt like she had to say it to convince everyone to allow the show to come to the island."

"I'm all for you and Tippy…"

"Not a thing, Dad," I interrupt.

"But I just can't wrap my head around why you'd want to be a part of that show. It crushed Jac."

I take a deep breath. I don't have an explanation. It's all just happened so quickly. I haven't had time to think. Tippy puts me in a different mindset. It's like she brainwashes me, and I don't think about real-world consequences. Not something I'm proud of.

"There are still a lot of ifs. If this comes to fruition, I will make sure we have revenge on that jackwagon Nick."

"Just be careful and thoughtful about what you're doing. Don't want anyone else to get hurt." Dad twirls the piece of grass in his mouth. "Shack looks good. Like what you've done."

"Tippy."

Dad chuckles. "She may be a good influence on you."

"No influencing going on here. Just taking what I can get from this deal." I open my front door and Dad stands up. To come in? Or leave?

"Matters of the heart aren't as obvious as you think, Dave. The more fight you put into this, the more feeling there must be."

Dad walks down the steps and gets in his Prius, and I walk into my house. Dad-isms. He's a man of few words, but the ones he speaks are folkloric.

GREENSEA GAZETTE

Islanders,

Well, that was a doozy! Tippy Meadowcroft had the audacity to enter Greensea into a reality show contest. Since the vote was nearly unanimous, we hope you're all doing your part and getting your bit of the island ready for its twenty seconds of fame.

The other big news was our newest Greensea couple! We're as shocked as you are, and we thought nothing got by us. Will there be wedding bells in store for our newest lovebirds? Only time will tell!

To the dads who rode tricycles onto the ferry...Dudes, what were you thinking?! You were correct when you told the ferry workers you weren't breaking any rules, but that's only because no one had dreamt that up yet. Rest assured, there will be a new rule from WSF tomorrow about man-powered three-wheeled vehicles. We think if you'd chosen something that moved at a quicker clip you could have gotten away with it, but all of your legs were way too long to make those things move quickly! Inquiring minds want to know where you rode them once you arrived in Seattle?

XOXO,

GG

CHAPTER SIXTEEN

TIPPY

Being seen around town is key to making this relationship look (and feel) real, so I ask Sylviane if she and Josh would meet us for dinner. Things still feel a little raw between Dave and me. I'm tiptoeing around, making sure this living together thing seems like less of an inconvenience and lasts as long as I need it to for the producers. They should have received the video, so we're just waiting for them to tell us when they'd like to come to Greensea for a visit.

Codmothers is Greensea's premier place for fish and chips. It's a little white clapboard restaurant down on Main Street, and it has a full house most nights of the week. Exactly why I picked it. We're guaranteed to see the most people if we're there.

"Let's take my car," says Dave.

I look down at my outfit. I'm wearing a white jumpsuit, and his truck will probably get me all dirty.

"It's old, not dirty. Get in. Thought there was some rule about wearing white before Memorial Day anyway."

"When you're Tippy Meadowcroft, you wear what you

want when you want."

White makes my hair pop—actually anything makes my hair pop—but this outfit fits like a glove, hugging all the right places. If I'm out with Dave, the least I can do is shine. And, plus, it's a power outfit, giving me all the confidence I need to take on the entire island if necessary.

I wipe the seat just in case and climb in. He's right, I'm surprised at how clean the truck is. I pictured oyster slop, but it's classy and vintage similar to my dad's convertible. Not even a single tear in the vinyl seats. We've yet to master the art of small talk with the quick change in our relationship status, so our drive is quiet.

Meadowcroft is just west and up the hill from Main Street. An easy five-minute drive. I roll the window down with the crank and let the wind blow through my curls. It rained all day, and the sun just came out.

Dave parks a couple of shops down from the restaurant. Since it's not busy season, parking spots downtown are aplenty. My bicep gets a good workout trying to crank up the window.

In the distance, Josh and Sylviane walk down the street. They're arm in arm, deep in conversation, not noticing anything around them, and my heart jumps with a pang of jealousy. I want that. Someone whose eyes light up when they hear me speak. Not someone I've tricked into spending time with me. My jealousy mixes with a bit of guilt about the situation we find ourselves in. At least I didn't steal Dave away from anyone. He'd just be at home sitting on his porch. Plus, I'm giving his business and his shack a chance to shine. There's a hint of a smile underneath his five o'clock shadow. Maybe he's not as ticked about this arrangement. But then again, maybe he's planning my demise.

"What's that look for?" asks Dave.

"What look?"

"You were wistful. Lost in thought."

"How do you even know what that word means?" I ask. He's an oyster farmer, not a professor.

"I'm not an idiot." He looks at me, and goes on. "What do you think? Me caveman. Me dig shells."

To be honest, I don't give Dave much credit. He carries around a bucket of seawater. I don't know what he studied in college. I have a vague recollection of seeing him at National Honor Society meetings in high school. And he was in a lot of my classes, which must mean he could keep up with me in school.

"Just because someone works with their hands doesn't mean they're stupid."

He gets out of the truck and walks over to open my door. He shoves his hands in the front pockets of his jeans, halfway between Bashful and Grumpy on the scale of cartoon characters.

"Sorry. That wasn't fair." I take a deep breath and say, "Maybe you can tell me more about the shells you work with sometime."

Dave ignores me, and we walk to Codmothers where Sylviane and Josh have already taken a seat at a table near the window.

"Wow! You dressed up!" says Sylviane.

Sylviane had a hard time getting used to the PNW style of dress. It took her months to stop wearing flip-flops on the trails. Spaghetti straps and tank tops were her M.O. until she realized the dark and cold had a way of cutting right through to your soul. She's wearing an oversized wool sweater and a floral skirt—probably a dress—with two little clips on the right side of her blonde bob.

"Well, this is a date, isn't it?" I ask. If I keep saying it, we will all believe it. "Although I know all white is a dangerous color when you're around." Harkening back to the time she honked her car horn, scaring me and causing me to spill on my exercise clothes.

"Touché," says Sylviane.

"Brother," says Josh.

"Brother," says Dave.

"Weirdos," I respond. "Is that how you always greet each other?"

Dave picks up the menu and Josh takes a sip of water.

"Nah," says Josh. "Only when an occasion calls for a little more awkwardness."

Dave, Josh, and I have known each other our whole lives. But I've rarely spent time with the two of them like this. It's like putting on your favorite sock and realizing it has a hole. Comfy yet nagging and uncomfortable.

Our server comes to the table and takes our order. The guys get appetizers, and Sylviane and I opt for a cup of soup before our main course.

Josh and Dave are laughing at some inside joke about their brother Oliver. I want to be a part of it, so I give Dave's shoulder a little push and let out a loud guffaw. Which is out of place and forces the three of them to look at me like I have a piece of spinach stuck in my teeth. Thankfully, the server appears with our drinks and our starters.

"Hope that's a double for you," says Sylviane, looking at me.

I'm not sure more alcohol is what I need. I swirl the cocktail stirrer around in my drink, trying to keep myself busy.

"Nice mussels, Dave," says Sylviane.

"He's my date, Sylviane. Not yours." I glare at her as I lift a spoonful of soup to my mouth.

Sylviane gives me a side-eye. "And?"

"Duh! It's rude to compliment his physique when I'm sitting right next to him."

What if the table next to us heard her? Then people might question the legitimacy of our relationship more than they already are.

"Tip, she's talking about the food on my plate," answers Dave.

Mussels. Not muscles. What is my problem? I tap my wrist ten times. Another calming technique I saw on Instagram last night. Why am I acting like this?

"Yeah, of course. I knew that." I stuff an oversized piece of bread in my mouth so I can't say anything else. After I'm done chewing, I wash the bread down with a large sip of my vodka and cranberry juice.

"Did you take something before we left the house?" asks Dave.

"Take something?" I ask.

"Yeah, like a 'shroom or some LSD?"

Josh sits back and crosses his arms like he's watching musical theatre...or maybe the circus.

"What are you talking about? I don't do drugs!"

"I don't know. Maybe you microdose or something." One side of Dave's mouth turns up.

"Why on earth would you think that?"

"Because. You're acting weird. Between that little shove, then the cackle, and the mussels freak out, there's really no accounting for your behavior." He pulls a mussel from its shell and slurps it off his fork. There's a twinkle in his eye. He's happiest when we're sparring.

Get it together, Tippy. Diaphragmatic breathing. Box breathing. Anything. More tapping. Just act like a regular human out with her friends.

"For your information, I haven't taken Fake Dating 101, so I'm not as skilled as you are in this little sham."

Sylviane and Josh are sitting back in their chairs like a pair of judges ready to flip over their score cards.

"Just curious, what was your plan if you didn't have me? How were you going to show off all these dates without someone on your arm?" asks Dave.

I stop and think for a second. "I would have brought Sylviane. She could have been my date. Or I would have gone alone. Having a guy around isn't the only way to prove something's romantic."

Dave eats another mussel and nods his head. "Maybe you set this whole thing up. You know darn well that it wouldn't have shown the romantic nature of any of those places if you were on your own. I think you figured out you needed a guy, and I was the closest victim."

I feel the heat start at my neck, and I'm certain my cheeks are turning crimson. "Dave Sherman! You know I did not set this up!" I go to cover up my red cheeks but hit the table, knocking my drink over, and I'm not able to catch it before it trickles down to my white jumpsuit.

"I'd like everyone to acknowledge that I had nothing to do with that," says Sylviane.

"Same," says Dave.

The server walks over with a towel, wipes the rest of my drink up, and has the busser bring me another. Which is good, because I need it.

I channel my best behavior for the rest of the night, which means I sit, eat my food, and nod. So I'm the opposite of the turmoil going on inside my head. Enough islanders came through and saw us, though. Mr. Crenshaw and his grandson are two tables away. Nora Cunningham sits with a young couple—new buyers, probably—at the bar. And Laura Prescott is on a date with someone tall, dark, and handsome.

Dinner ends without further incident and we say goodnight. I hear Sylviane and Josh giggle as they walk down the street to their car. Dave and I are quiet again on the ride home. This time I keep my window closed and look straight ahead. We pull in the driveway and go into the house, exchanging no conversation. My entire system is overloaded. I need some sensory deprivation.

"I'm going to take a bath. See you in the morning."

I race into my bedroom and close the door, leaving Dave in my dust.

I'm not used to having houseguests. If a relative comes to visit, they stay with Mom and Dad. A few girlfriends from college stay with me once or twice a year, but never a guy. And never someone moving in with me without a departure date. I need some quiet. Some time to think about the show and how I'm going to act when the producers are here. Maybe I do need to take some drugs to calm myself down. Mental note to go to The Corner Joint tomorrow to see if they have anything that can help me.

After turning the tub faucet on and grabbing some bath salts, I get undressed, laying my stained jumpsuit on my bed. The water feels good. I lean my head back and let all the stress fall out of my body. Tomorrow will be easier.

My big dreams of falling for a producer on the show, or one of the contestants realizing I'm the woman of his dreams, won't happen while I have Dave living with me. I might as well have *not available* tattooed on my forehead. I'm postponing everything until the show's over. Maybe I'd be better off telling everyone the truth and taking my chances. Andrew said he liked a compelling backstory. What's more compelling than a fake dating trope in real life?

My skin prunes, so I get out and grab my robe off the back of the door. It's quiet in the rest of the house so I walk out to make a cup of tea. A little chamomile before bed is just what the doctor ordered.

CHAPTER SEVENTEEN

DAVE

Tippy must've gone to bed right after her bath. I don't hear her moving around. I sneak out of the room and go down the hall to the kitchen. There's a soft glow from a nightlight, like the house has been tucked in. Codmothers didn't fill me up, and my stomach's growling for my late-night chocolate. She's got to have some in one of these cabinets. Tippy's standing right at the sink in a short white robe. Is everything of hers white? The robe's slipped off one of her shoulders.

"Hey," I say in a calm voice, so I don't scare her like Bear did to me earlier. She turns around, holding her mug and a tea bag. And I realize the robe's slipped down in the front, revealing one side of her bare chest, so I look away. Tippy notices and looks down, dropping her mug on the hardwood floor as she races to pull her robe closed.

"Don't move. You're barefoot." At least I still have my shoes on.

"Broom's in the front closet," she says.

I run to get it. When I get back with the broom and the dustpan, she's bent down picking up the big pieces of the mug. She doesn't even look up, but her robe is practically tied around her like a straitjacket.

"Can we pretend this never happened?" she asks.

"I'd like nothing better." We clean up in silence.

I want to forget I saw Tippy partially naked, but I can't because it's making me crazy inside. Her red curls hanging over her shoulder, running across the top of her lightly freckled chest, and I want nothing more than to take her robe off and uncover the rest of her. But I can't let my mind go there. So I sing the song I sing when I can't fall asleep.

"One little, two little, three little oysters. Four little, five little, six little sea creatures."

Tippy stands up, looks at me, and raises her eyebrows. "Are we back in preschool?"

"Just doing what you asked...pretending nothing happened."

She sighs, shakes her head, throws the big pieces away, and heads to her bedroom, slamming the door.

I finish cleaning up and get ready for bed. How the hell is this going to work? How can we be in close quarters like this? And most importantly, why do I want to devour that girl? She's Tippy. Tippy Freaking Meadowcroft. Don't think about the curve of her shoulder, or how her hair would feel nuzzled into your neck. Dave! Get a hold of yourself! I go to the bathroom and splash my face with cold water, get into bed, and sing my oyster song to clear my head.

———

I'm bringing some of my precious creatures over to Tippy's. I feel like I might be able to pretend the little slip of the robe never happened if we're sharing some oysters on the half shell.

Maybe. She did say she wanted to learn more about what I do, and tonight's the perfect opportunity.

The French doors are open, and Tippy's sitting at a wood table on her patio. Her view is peaceful. Nothing but evergreen trees on three sides of her house.

"Hey," I yell from the kitchen, so I don't scare her and start off on the wrong foot again. "What are you up to?" I plate the oysters so at least my presentation will be decent.

"Not much, but I heard from *Love at the Last Resort*, and they'll be here the day after tomorrow."

"Whoa! That was fast!" I bring my plate, some little forks, and some chutney out to the patio.

She turns and looks at me. There's a softness in her eyes I haven't seen before. Maybe it's because we're usually ready to spar, but now we're attempting to get along. The barely spring air is cool. Tippy's bundled in a fleece and a knit hat.

"What do you have?"

"Brought you some oysters." I set the plate on the table in front of her.

"You're not going to start your little preschool singing act again, are you?" She smiles.

"Depends on if you do some kind of striptease or not."

Her cheeks flush. I plan to sing in my head as soon my mind wanders back to the slip of the robe.

"Don't you know I don't eat oysters?" she says as I take a seat at the table.

"I'm convinced you haven't had any as good as mine."

They say plants grow better when you talk to them, and the same is true for oysters. That's why mine are superb.

"Let me clarify, I haven't had any before."

Stop the presses! "You mean to tell me you've never tried one of these delectable treats? I thought you just didn't like them. I didn't know that you haven't had any."

Challenge accepted.

"Nope. I don't eat slime," says Tippy.

I take a deep breath. No one calls my oysters slime. She hasn't forgotten how to make my benevolent feelings disappear.

"Bivalves are not slime. You have a pillow that says, 'The World is Your Oyster,' for chrissakes!" It's sitting in the center of her couch.

"My grandmother needlepointed that thing decades ago, and it's a common idiom, not a profession of love."

My jaw's tightening and my eyebrows are furrowing. She exasperates me. "And if you're 'dating' an oyster farmer, the TV people are going to expect you to be invested in my oysters. It's in your best interest to like them, or at least pretend to."

She stares at me. "Remember, no threats."

"It's not a threat. Merely a suggestion. You can't force me to smile and look like I'm having fun. I could just walk around looking miserable all the time. I could be the ball and chain you're forcing me to be. Or I could look lovingly into your eyes."

I flutter my eyelashes and rub my hands through my too-short hair.

"All I have to do is eat one?"

"Just one, because I know you won't be able to resist eating more after you taste the briny flavor of my oysters."

She stares at the plate of freshly shucked shells in front of her.

"I don't even know how to do it!"

She stretches her arms out like she's about to bend down and pick one up with her mouth.

"Ah, Tip? We're not bobbing for apples."

"I don't know. Like, am I supposed to pick them up with my hands?"

"Yes!"

She reaches down in a pincer grab, and this time she looks like she's about to pick the oyster up without its shell.

"Have you ever watched anyone eat one before?"

"I don't really pay attention to things like that, and I don't like to eat anything complicated. A taco is about as finger food as I get."

I hand her a cocktail fork.

"Some people use a fork, but I like when they slide into my mouth." I take one, tilt the shell toward my mouth. Give it a gentle suck. And the oyster slips in. This one's sweet with a hint of fresh salt. I can taste the sea in the best way. I close my eyes as it rolls down my throat. It's as close to a religious experience as I want to have. She's staring at me when I open my eyes.

"You should eat that behind closed doors, Dave. Or at least with the blinds down."

I hand her the fork, and I spoon a little of my fresh cocktail chutney in the shell's corner. The tomato jam will hide the texture and the taste until she's used to it.

"Your turn."

Tippy pokes the oyster with her fork. All the chutney falls into the shell. Mission not accomplished with that. She closes her eyes, lifts the shell to her mouth, and tries to take a bite of what's on her fork, but can't, because no one bites an oyster. First rule of oyster eating: swallow it whole.

She spits out the part that was in her mouth and drops the shell, which lands at her feet, just missing her fuzzy boots.

"I can't do it!" Tippy wails.

"Well, no one in the history of the world eats it like you're trying to. Do it in one bite. Just suck it down."

"Suck it down? I don't suck anything down!"

I can't help it when my eyes go wide and I start imagining too many other things.

"Get your mind out of the gutter, Dave. I meant food."

"Better figure out how to eat one, Tip, or you might blow the little Tippy and Dave Go to Hollywood charade."

Tears well up in her eyes, but I can tell it's fake. If anyone bats their eyes that many times, they're sure to get teary.

"Just do it," I coax.

She thinks about it. Pours about a tablespoon of chutney on one. Picks up the shell and tilts it back. I watch her open her smooth pink lips just wide enough for the shell. She slides her tongue up and sucks the oyster down. I watch her swallow and realize why she told me to take it behind closed doors. One little, two little, three little oysters.

She ends with a gag, which feels like a cold splash of water waking me from my reverie of Tippy Freaking Meadowcroft.

"Really?" I shake my head. "It's not that bad." Just like Tippy to add a little flourish at the end.

"I did it. Happy now? You didn't say I had to actually like it." She slams the shell down on the plate.

I take one for myself and suck it down. I can't believe I got even the littlest bit of pleasure watching her eat one. I don't know what's happening to me. It's like the years and years of rivalry and joking around have slipped away with the slip of her robe. If I'm honest with myself, it's like the first bullseye she got on our date pierced something in my heart.

"Better figure it out before Mr. TV Man gets here. Won't be believable if you're dating an oyster guy and hate oysters."

"As far as I can see, that's the least of our problems," she sighs.

Least of our problems, is right. I'm catching a cold in the form of feelings. There's something stirring inside of me, and I just can't shake it. Her sighs and the eye rolls remind me that she's not feeling the same way. I'm the same old Dave who's been bugging her since the beginning of time.

Tippy takes a notebook from next to her in the chair.

"Okay," she says, freeing me from my mind. "First question...Just want to make sure we're both on the same page if we have to touch each other or, umm, kiss, or anything."

I squint and look at her, not sure what she's getting at.

"We're both giving consent to the other person to act in the moment like we're dating, right?"

I think for a second. "Yes, I give you consent to do whatever you'd like to me." Can't help but crack a smile.

Tippy rolls her eyes. "And I give you consent to do what's necessary." She goes on like we're not talking about something really important. "We'll take the 7:05 ferry over to the city to meet the producer and take the 8:10 right back. We'll go right for a cinnamon roll and a cup of coffee. Then we'll take them here, Meadowcroft, and play a round of pickleball."

"Whoa. No way. I'm not playing that stupid game again."

"I ate an oyster. You don't have a choice anymore."

"You're a glutton for punishment, it seems." I smile.

"Well, hopefully you'll be more careful."

"What if we just volley for a little while tonight? We'll have the net in between us so I can't accidentally deck you."

"Good plan. Let's go over the rest of the day first."

I nod along as she goes through the play-by-play.

Islanders,

Stop the presses! Have you seen Greensea Goat? Someone has touched up the rock and given her a fresh coat of paint. A much needed one, we might add. But this column has received 167 emails concerning the color the goat was painted. So we set out to investigate. Previously, Greensea Goat was painted with white deck paint and the furry chin section was Toasted Nutmeg. Currently, it has been painted Toasted Marshmallow in outdoor latex and the chin is Burnt Sienna. Is it different? No question. But we challenge you to let us know why it matters! Who cares if Greensea Goat is a different color? Does it affect your life? No! Let's talk about things that make a difference in your day and not these things that don't matter.

Just a friendly reminder that our special guests will be on the island today! We hope you're all on your best behavior...Do not, and we repeat, please do not spray paint another landmark. And if you see Tippy and Dave walking around with the TV people, be sure to put on your biggest smile.

XOXO,

GG

CHAPTER EIGHTEEN

TIPPY

Kirk, our faithful newspaper salesman who has mastered the art of staring into potential customers' souls and forcing them to buy a paper, waits for every passenger to walk onto the ferry. He never says a word but somehow gets people to make a purchase. Even me, the owner's daughter, who should never have to buy a paper. Especially since I've already read it. But I buy my requisite copy and board the ferry with Dave to meet Melinda.

There's a little wind, giving the Sound a few whitecaps, reminding me I'm on a floating vessel. I love the routine of the ferry. Waiting in line for the announcement to board. I always buck the crowd, entering on the starboard side of the boat and walking to my table in the galley. A two-top table with twirly chairs instead of the four seater, as it reduces the risk of someone else sitting next to us. When I sit in a big booth, there's always a chance someone will pull up on the other vinyl bench. And I reserve my conversations for special, invited people only. Today, Dave is that person.

On a normal day, the galley gives me prime viewing. Watching what everyone buys and eats. Who goes back for a second ferry pour of wine. Who buys the tater tots because they believe calories don't count on ferries. And who's posing in a booth for their new Tinder profile. I see it all from my seat in the galley, but today my mission is to make sure Dave and I are seen by as many people as possible.

I've memorized Melinda Sanchez's resume. I know she graduated from Boston College magna cum laude. Moved to Hollywood and interned on *The Bachelor*. Worked her way up the network ladder. Like me, she has one older brother, and her parents have settled down and retired in the hills of Marin County. I scoured the web to get as much info as I could, but her social media presence is pretty locked down, other than a Taylor Swift post she liked in 2015.

When I hear the first strum of the banjo, I sit up straight in my seat. Today is too important to leave anything to chance. It's too early for that bold busker to be on the ferry playing his tunes. It's one thing to do it on a jovial Friday evening, but seven AM is not the time. This is the regular commuter boat, for goodness' sake. People are working. Some are on video calls. I look at Dave, who looks like a deer in headlights, and I stomp over and stand in front of the banjo player until he has to stop.

"What do you think you're doing?" I ask.

"Playing my banjo, ma'am." He's wearing a flannel and has a much-too-long strawberry blond beard.

"Don't ma'am me! This is not the time or place for your music."

"According to city statute 14-876, musicians are free to play their music from seven AM until ten PM in public spaces, and according to state statute 7132, the ferry is a state-run public space. So I may play whatever I want."

A well-versed busker. Interesting.

"Out of common courtesy for fellow riders, stop."

"According to city statute 14-877, the music must be under 70 decibels, and I've placed a decibel meter right here to make sure my banjo stays at the appropriate level."

Checkmate. This guy knows his stuff. And if he's going this way, he's not going the other way. I feel a hand on my arm and turn to see Dave.

"Let's go for a walk," he suggests, trying to diffuse the situation.

"Good idea. We can grab some selfies for the 'gram." I lead the way to the deck. Perfect timing. The sun's peaking above the Cascade Mountains, and Mt. Rainier glows pink.

"Your arms are longer." I hand Dave my phone and lean my head into his.

Dave takes a few pictures, but my hair's blowing out of control. He spits some of it out of his mouth.

"Gross! You didn't have to do that!"

"Your hair's in my mouth. What did you expect me to do? Eat it?"

So much for a romantic picture on the boat.

———

Melinda is standing in the terminal when we disembark the boat.

"Melinda." I stick my hand out. "Tippy Meadowcroft. So nice to meet you in person."

"Good morning, Tippy!" She reaches in for a hug.

"I think you remember Dave in the background of our meeting." I gesture to Dave, who offers his hand right away.

"Nice to meet you, Melinda! Can't wait to show you our island." His acting skills are above par.

"Hi!" Melinda returns the handshake with both of her hands gripping his. "So glad to meet a real PNW man."

She's starry eyed behind her cat-eye glasses. I look at Dave. He fits the bill for lumbersexual. Tight-fitted flannel shirt with a crisp white undershirt peeking out. Clean, dark jeans paired with well-worn Blundstone boots. He's topped it off with a knit hat over his closely shorn hair. And he's left just enough stubble to look intriguing rather than lazy.

"You okay, Tip?" Dave asks, nudging me out of my reverie and toward the entrance to the ferry.

"I've never been on a ferry before! I'm quite excited!" At least Melinda didn't notice my staring. Or at least, she didn't think anything of it.

I snap back into reality, hand Melinda her ticket, and motion for her to follow me. It's still a rush hour ferry even though we're going back to the island, so there are quite a few people. I put my QR code on the screen and the little gates open. Melinda does the same.

We walk down the loading bridge and board the ferry. Melinda looks around.

"Wow! It's so much bigger than I expected! I thought it'd be more like a tour boat."

Of course I direct us right back to the galley, but a four top this time.

"Can I get you anything? Cup of coffee?" Dave asks, pointing toward the galley. Add gentleman to the qualities he's brought with him today.

"No, I'm fine. Just excited to get a feel for the people on Greensea!"

"Well, remember, anyone could be on this boat! They're not all islanders!" I make a blanket statement that will cover us from any fools.

The safety announcement begins and we're on our way when I hear the banjo again. It's a crisp whine, more like a crying toddler than music. I turn to look and it's the same guy playing his banjo, but this time he's in a crowd. You've got to be kidding me. Someone taps a bucket. Another person gets out a recorder. What in the hell! It has to be the first time a recorder has been used outside of a fourth grade classroom.

"Melinda, please excuse me for one second." I smile sweetly and Dave takes over the conversation while I walk over to the makeshift band.

"Are you kidding me?" I whisper-yell to the original banjo player, trying not to let Melinda see how mad I am.

"Hi again, ma'am. Didn't expect you to be on the ferry," he says, still strumming.

"Right back at you, but I believe you're breaking the codes you recited earlier. Surely the collective noise is greater than what's allowed."

"Actually, according to city ordinance..."

I put my hand out. "Stop! How much will it take to get you to put the instruments away? We don't need to look like the Bad News Bears right now."

The musicians look at each other. The guy tapping on the bucket mouths something to the banjo player, and he shakes his head and sticks his thumb up in a motion indicating "go higher."

"Thirty..."

Another guy speaks up. "Fifty bucks."

I open my bag. "Do you take Venmo?"

He shakes his head and strums his banjo, and I whip out a fifty and walk away for the second time this morning. But I stop mid-turn.

"Where are you all headed?"

"Gazebo on Main Street," says the man with the recorder.

No way! Not on my watch. I pull out my phone and text Mayor Nickerbottom.

> Tippy: Mayor, a dozen buskers on the ferry coming to play at the gazebo. Must stop them as the Love at the Last Resort producer is on the ferry with me. We do not need Greensea to look like the Island of Misfits anymore than it already does.
>
> Mayor: Good morning to you too, Tippy. According to city ordinance...

I can't read anymore.

> Tippy: I don't care about any of the stupid ordinances. Today is the day we have to put our best foot forward. If you want extra tourist dollars, and my support in your next campaign, stop them or you'll be sorry.

He doesn't respond, which makes me certain he'll do what he can to make sure nothing embarrassing happens.

I walk back and join Dave and Melinda, who is holding her head up with one hand on the table.

"Are you okay?" I ask. She's green around the edges.

"Sea sick. Is it always this rocky?"

No it isn't, but short of paying the waves to dial it back, there's nothing I can do.

"Let's move over to the chairs in the back. It'll be better if you stare straight at the horizon."

I take her bag and Dave leads the way. She can put her head back and stare in the direction we're moving. I get her situated and send Dave to the galley to grab some ginger ale. I can still hear the band members yucking it up with snacks on me. Hopefully that's the end of them. Don't need a jalopy of a band making their way to Main Street before I show our fair island off to Melinda.

The ride smooths out as we pull into the harbor, but Melinda doesn't look any better. I whisper to Dave to get off first and pull the car down to pick us up at the entrance.

CHAPTER NINETEEN

Melinda looks at me as we walk into the Greensea terminal and whispers, "Is there a bathroom?"

"Yes, yes. Right here." I point to the rudimentary bathrooms in the ferry terminal. The terminal itself is smaller than a fast-food restaurant, with only bathrooms and a dozen seats inside.

She rushes over.

"Can I take your bag for you?" I offer, but she's already in the bathroom, and it would be awkward to just follow her in there.

Shit. She's more than a little motion sick. Could it be food poisoning? I lean up against the wall and wait for her to emerge.

"I'm sorry," Melinda says when she finally comes out of the bathroom.

"Still seasick?" I ask.

"Yes. I thought I'd be fine on a larger boat, but that definitely was not the case."

"Do you need to lie down? Want to sit for a minute?"

"No, no. I'll be fine after I get some fresh air."

We walk outside and Dave's out of the car yelling into another car. What the hell is he doing?

"Dave. Dave!" I try to be inconspicuous, but she'd have to be blind and deaf not to see him yelling and me trying to get his attention. Good thing he made a positive impression earlier.

"Tip, hurry. Mr. Aarons over here is hot and bothered because I've been parked for more than the allotted two minutes."

There are strict rules about parking in front of the ferry terminal. I'm surprised Dave didn't pull into a spot to wait, but I have to make light of it all. I have a sick producer to impress.

"Here, Melinda, why don't you take the front seat. We're going less than a mile, but it should help with the motion sickness."

She climbs in the car and puts her head back on the headrest.

"Sorry about that," he says. "Crotchety old islander."

Dave laughs a little too hard, and I hope he feels the lasers from my eyes burning a hole in the back of his head.

"No worries," says Melinda.

"Roll down Melinda's window for some fresh air, Dave," I say.

I hold my breath when we pull down Main Street and pass the gazebo, only to see a perfectly placed circle of preschoolers playing the newly popular game Prius, Prius, Tesla. Score one for Mayor Nickerbottom. No one can kick a bunch of four-year-olds out of the town green to play their music. Nicely done. I need the win right now.

Our first stop is Apollo for the best cinnamon rolls in the state. People take the ferry from all over just to have a roll ever since some TikToker put them on the map.

Dave finds a spot right in front, and we all get out of the car.

Melinda takes a deep breath, trying to keep her nausea at bay. Dave opens the door and we walk in.

"Oh my goodness. It smells heavenly in here."

Score! She's happy and she's right. The air is filled with the scent of fresh cinnamon and sugar. Slightly yeasty dough. And just a hint of saltwater. I've always thought they should make a candle.

"Try their cinnamon rolls. They're simply the best," I say.

"Are they gluten-free?" asks Melinda.

"Of course not!" says Dave. "They're filled with so much gluten you can taste it from Seattle."

"Oh darn, I only eat gluten-free food."

For crying out loud. If we're counting strikes, I'm in trouble. I try to hide my frustration. "Let's just grab a coffee then and go over to Bowls on the Bay for an acai bowl or a yogurt parfait," I suggest.

Dave slumps his shoulders. "I was looking forward to this sugary goodness."

"There's no reason you can't have one," says Melinda. "I'm sure Tippy wants to keep her man satisfied."

My man. Right. I pet his arm.

"Honey boo, get one. You know I don't care."

Dave smirks. Honey boo. Yes, that's the best I could come up with.

"Thanks, snookems."

Dave pets my arm in return and gets in line, while Melinda and I go back outside. The air will be good for her, and with the luck I'm having this morning, she'll probably go into anaphylactic shock if she inhales too much gluten.

"How'd you two meet?" Melinda asks.

"Hmm...I don't remember the first time we met," I say, thinking back. Our moms probably pushed us around the park in strollers together. Or maybe we were in grocery carts at

Island Grocers, and we met in the frozen food aisle. Dave Sherman has always been around in my life.

"One of those relationships?" asks Melinda. "Met while you were wearing your beer goggles?"

"No! We were babies. Maybe toddlers. Dave and I have known each other for as long as I can remember."

"Really? So were you middle school sweethearts?"

"No!"

"Then how'd you start dating?"

I've thought of everything. Planned out every detail of this day down to the socks I'm wearing, when we play pickleball, and what time we should arrive at the General's house to get the best view of the sunset, but I never thought to come up with an answer to that question. Thankfully Dave comes out of Apollo with his cinnamon roll before I have to answer. He looks like the cat who caught the canary, savoring every bite of his breakfast.

"Shall we walk over to get us some food?" I ask.

Dave nods and we cross the street.

Main Street is doing its best to show off. The store windows are all done up. Between the Covers has a display of local authors. Island Grocers set up a little farm stand in the parking lot. Greensea is oozing charm from every orifice.

"Dave, I was just asking Tippy how you two started dating."

"Oh, look!" I say, trying to distract them. There's no way Dave's come up with an answer to that question if I haven't. "The peacock." Fortunately, the peacock is crossing the street, feathers on full display.

Dave ignores me and answers. "I knew there was something between us after I watched her eat an oyster," says Dave, not skipping a beat.

"Oh, tell me more!" says Melinda.

"She attacked that thing like it was going to eat her alive. Like the little, harmless, opalescent piece of goodness was a threat to her. Stabbed it with her fork. Dipped it in some sauce. And swallowed it down." He stops and I swallow the fumes coming up my throat. He's making me sound like a person with a grudge against sea animals. "She went at it full throttle. Like she does every single thing in her life. I knew right then and there that I needed her energy in my life in a different way than I'd ever had before."

"That's so romantic," says Melinda.

I stop in the middle of the sidewalk. Wait. What? Does he really need my energy? I look at Dave. He's smiling and walking straight ahead. Did he really feel that way after he watched me eat his creature, or is he just an amazing actor? No. Stop. Fake. The whole goal of today is faking our relationship. Don't fall for it, Tippy. He just spit your hair out of his mouth less than an hour ago.

"Is that when you caught feelings for him?"

I snap the ponytail holder around my wrist to bring myself back down to earth.

"Actually, yes. He had sauce dripping down his chin, and I went to wipe it off and I felt the electricity pulsing between us."

Melinda laughs. "You guys are something else."

I wink at him when Melinda turns her back.

We pass the window display at Greensea Pharmacy—dyed-green maxi pads shaped into clovers.

"Greensea is a vibe," says Melinda, looking around. "I think our audience would love to see all this quirkiness."

I take a deep breath. Maybe things aren't going as poorly as I thought. Maybe I'm just overthinking everything.

"I think I'd like to get a better feeling for the logistics. After we get a bite to eat, can we head out to the site where we'd have contestants stay?"

I rip up the schedule I made in my mind. I'd planned to be

at Swifterson at sunset, but I'm Tippy Meadowcroft and I'm adaptable.

"Absolutely." I nod to Dave, and we walk over to the Bowls on the Bay food truck parked right behind Island Grocers to get some açai bowls.

———

Swifterson House turned on all the charm today. The sun's shining and the water gleams in the background when we pull up. Melinda gets out of the car and takes a few pictures of the house from the circular driveway. It looks like something from *Gone With the Wind*. All white. Large pillars. Gorgeous millwork around the windows. A ferry passes by in the distance.

"Tippy, this place is stunning. It will look great on camera."

Cha-ching. Jackpot. Now maybe she'll overlook all that we'll need to do to the interior to make it livable.

I arranged for Ms. Smith to open the doors, let us in, and then leave so I can be the tour guide.

Melinda records the view as we walk through the front door into a foyer with a large crystal chandelier. Circular stairs line either side of the foyer. A parlor type room is to the left, and a living room is to the right. Straight back is the dining room lined with French doors facing the bay. The kitchen is in its own wing next to the dining room, separated by a swinging door. Oriental rugs and period pieces cover every inch of the house.

"We may want to change out the furnishings to something more lived-in and comfortable. More Pottery Barn and less Ethan Allen," says Melinda, who's pulled out a notebook and is taking copious notes.

"Of course. That won't be a problem." I take out my pad of paper and write *RENT FURNITURE*. Dave's mom, Barb, worked for a realty company and will help me find someone to stage the house. Coupled with my mom's decorating, it will be top-tier.

"Keep in mind, there's a bunkhouse next to this property, so the men can stay there. The bedrooms in here will be for the women."

We walk up the stairs to the five bedrooms. Each has a small bathroom. A primary bedroom has a full ensuite with a soaking tub. The beds are all poster, and each room has a dresser. But the most showstopping feature of the house is the sweeping view.

An eagle soars in the distance and a light breeze moves through the trees. Swifterson put on its Sunday best for this visit.

"I plan on changing all the beds to bunk beds. Each room should be able to hold two sets of bunks," I explain to Melinda. She nods her head and writes something down.

"Let's go out back," suggests Dave.

We walk down the stairs and open the French doors onto a stone patio. I always thought this would be a perfect venue for a wedding. It's majestic. The back side of the house is as photogenic as the front, allowing for even better camera angles.

"We could set up a volleyball court and other lawn games," says Dave. "The property is fifteen acres, with trails that wander through the woods. There's a Japanese teahouse on the north side of the property. I think that might be the perfect spot to set up a little confessional or whatever you call it on the show."

I glance at Dave and my mouth hangs open. He's bringing it today. I hadn't even thought about that, but it's a perfect idea.

Melinda shivers. I offer her an extra cardigan I have in the car.

"The sea breeze can cut right through you. Always need to wear layers on Greensea," I say.

Dave runs to the car and grabs my sweater.

"This has potential," says Melinda. "Let's see the bunkhouse."

We walk down the path to the other house. There's an old stone pool that's never been filled up, as far as I can remember. It was a late addition to the property after the wars were over.

"Might be nice to fill this," says Dave. "I'll look into it."

I'd kiss him if only we weren't fake dating.

The bunkhouse is right next to the pool. It's dark and a little musty but nothing a few open windows can't take care of, and no one will notice when a dozen men and all their sweat are living in here. There's a foyer with a large wooden table. Doors on either side lead to bedrooms with four bunk beds in each. There are two bathrooms, locker room style, that sit behind the bedrooms. It's a campground that had a glow up.

Melinda nods again and takes more notes. I want to see what's on her college ruled notebook.

We drive by the Japanese teahouse on the way out. I forgot how beautiful this property is and how precious. Greensea is a gem, truly an emerald in the Puget Sound.

———

Since gluten is totally off the menu, we stop at my favorite—and the only—farm-to-table restaurant on Greensea, The Fork & Stable. We sit down in the farmhouse, a glorified barn. It's rustic but barn-chic. Chandeliers of fairy lights line the ceilings. Vintage tablecloths on every table. Mismatched napkins and silverware. It has a strong vibe. Bell spent a great deal of time consulting with the owners, Ash and Vic Willard, to make it all look just right. They tried hard to make it look like they didn't try at all.

Ash comes over to take our order just as Vic bangs the door open.

"Have you seen him?" Vic yells.

"Seen who?" asks Ash.

"Gus! He's on the loose again."

"Who's Gus?" Melinda asks tentatively.

"Baby goat," says Ash.

"There's a goat on the loose in the restaurant?" Melinda asks.

"Hopefully not in the restaurant, per se, but definitely somewhere on the property." Ash walks back to the kitchen.

Greensea-ers are used to things like this. Peacocks, llamas, pigs, horses. They turn up everywhere you're not expecting them. It's like animals on the island have an extra gene that urges them to be free and run about. This always shocks visitors. Some are horrified about the mix of animals and people. Others take selfies whenever they can. Albeit most of the time it feels like the best selfie opportunities are in the middle of the road, stopping traffic. But at least it's not like all the people in Yellowstone taking pictures with bison. Animals on Greensea won't gore you to death.

Melinda has her notebook out again, and I can't imagine what she's writing this time. Just as she sets her pen down, a pan clatters and the door to the kitchen flies open. Ash is yelling, "I'll make a stew out of you!" A goat, presumably Gus, runs through the dining room right to the sunlight coming from the windows. The doors to the outside don't push open, they require a turn of a knob, causing Gus to be stuck. He makes a little "maa" noise and chases his tail, running around in circles next to the door. Dave stands up, drops his Indian block napkin on the table, and goes after Gus.

"Here, goaty, goaty. Come here, Gus." He's crouched down, moving slowly, like he's calling a cat. Is this an effective way to call a goat too? I look at Melinda. Her eyes are wide and her mouth's hanging open. She doesn't look scared, but who would be of this tiny creature? Just a bit of shock and awe on her face. Gus stops and looks at Dave. His nose moves like he's smelling whether or not Dave is friendly. Dave gets closer and closer and then lunges toward him, picking him up and cradling him in his arms just as Vic blasts through the kitchen door.

"Gosh darn little critter! Thank you, Dave!"

"Better fix the hole in the pen if you want to keep him in one place," says Dave, handing the goat over.

"This little runt can sneak through the tiniest openings, that's for sure. He thinks he belongs inside because he gets to come in to do goat yoga. Poor guy's confused! You mind looking at the fence and helping me while you wait for your lunch? Won't be but a minute, and I'm sure Ash will comp your meal for you."

Dave looks at me and I nod. Melinda and I could use a moment to discuss what she's seen so far. And I can try to convince her the island isn't a walking petting zoo.

"Isn't he a jack of all trades," says Melinda, watching Dave walk outside.

"He sure is." I'm not sure if she means it as a compliment or if she's rolling her eyes in her head.

"Like a prince on his white horse," she says, practically making googly eyes at the door.

Not sure I'd go that far. But she seems to think Dave's a good specimen, so at least we have that going for us.

Ash brings our salads and Dave's burger. He's still not back yet, but we eat without him.

"Thought we could play a little pickleball next before we go out to dinner and get you back on the ferry."

"I've never played, but it is all the rage."

"Well, you know, Greensea is the birthplace of the sport," I say and launch into my well-rehearsed history of pickleball. "I'm sure you'll pick it up in no time."

"Maybe easier than goat yoga?"

"Goat yoga is just stretching and petting baby goats. I don't think anyone uses it as serious exercise."

"Don't they get the heebie jeebies with animals crawling on them?"

"I guess the people who don't like animals don't go to goat yoga."

"It's so different here from LA." Melinda takes a bite of her salad. "People here seem more real and not caught up in what they look like. Is there even a place to get Botox?"

We may look real, but there's a fair amount of Botox and other enhancements that take place on the island. I guess we just go for a little pick-me-up, while people in LA go for wrinkle free like a pressed shirt.

"There is. Greensea has everything you might want." I'm lying through my teeth. We don't have a lot of things, but the good old market has expanded their offerings to granny panties and boxer shorts. Island Grocers has a couple of plain white tees, and Cedar & Fern is carrying more than just farmwear. But that online retailer everyone loves to hate is an islander's best friend with twenty-four-hour delivery.

"I like the pace of the island. Everything seems a little slower. I swear, in LA everyone is running to and from something. And the traffic! Certainly more relaxing to take a boat. Do you have Pilates and yoga without animals on the island?"

"Of course! Our Pilates studio, The Reformation, is top-notch. I ride my bike there most mornings."

"Wow! Impressive on these hills."

I intentionally didn't mention it's an e-bike.

"What else could Greensea offer for *Love at the Last Resort*?"

Jackpot. Best question ever. I go on about all the things to do on the island while we wait for Dave to return. Golf at Thin

Pines with cocktails from the infamous drink cart. Renting paddleboards from Cedar & Fern and SUPing in Pickles Harbor. Dates in the city with romantic ferry rides. Sunset picnics at Gulls Point. I cover all the bases.

Dave comes back in a completely fresh shirt and pants.

"What happened to you?"

"You don't want to know. Vic lent me some clothes."

He smells like a fresh bar of soap as he sits down to eat his burger.

"Sorry about that," he says with a mouth half full of burger.

"No worries," says Melinda. "Pretty impressive the way you caught him."

Dave waves it off.

CHAPTER TWENTY

DAVE

This day has been nothing like what I expected so far, but it's pretty easy to impress Melinda, and the island is cooperating. We drive to Meadowcroft to bounce around a ball on the pickleball court. Tippy's hard selling the sport.

"Playing pickleball on screen will bring many new viewers who have not seen *Love at the Last Resort* previously but have a great deal of interest in the sport. The ratings will shoot through the roof."

Melinda shakes her head and takes out her little Nancy Drew pad of paper. She must be writing a dissertation on Greensea. I'd give anything to see what she has written on that notebook.

Bell has a thermos of tea and an assortment of pickleball themed sugar cookies set out on a table for us. Tippy hands a cup to Melinda and I'm guessing Tippy wasn't able to send a message to Bell that Melinda was gluten free. More cookies for me.

"Why don't you two just show me how it's done," says Melinda.

Our track record leaves something to be desired, but as long as no one's injured or storms off the court, I'll consider it a victory.

Tippy and I head onto the court. I've been studying pickleball slang and watching videos so I don't embarrass myself.

"Why don't you serve first, Tip?"

She grabs a ball and yells, "Pickle!" before she serves.

I hit it back too softly. "Ugh, sorry. That was a falafel."

Tippy picks up the ball and looks at me for a second.

She serves again. I return it, giving it the nice requisite bounce. I yell, "Dillball!" after it bounces once. Tippy hits it back to me, and I call, "Flapjack," and hit it back, shouting, "Opa."

Tippy doesn't return it, even though she could have.

"Did you read the Urban Dictionary of Pickleball slang?"

"I just wanted to get up on all the lingo!"

Tippy shakes her head in disbelief and serves again.

Melinda laughs. My commentary tickles her. Take that! I'm scoring points all over the place! We play for a few more minutes and walk over to Melinda.

"Dave, you are a crack-up! I think people will have just as much fun watching the two of you as they will the rest of the show."

Tippy bites her lip. I pat her on the back a little harder than necessary. "We are pretty cute."

"This will be a great way for contestants to get to know each other. Kudos, Tippy! You have some great ideas!"

"She's full of them. I don't think there's anyone on the island, maybe in the state, better suited to plan things than Tippy Meadowcroft." I put my arm around her shoulders and pull her in for a squeeze. My elbow hits her shoulder at the perfect spot. Her hair tickles my arm, and I hope she doesn't feel my pulse quicken.

Tippy laughs and pushes me away. "I don't know if that's true," she says, but she smiles bigger than I've seen her. She's glowing. Is it because Melinda's happy and likes what she sees, or was it from my arm pulling her in?

———

Our last stop for the day is The Old Owl. We know Quinn is well versed in serving up options for those with dietary restrictions, and we need to ensure Melinda leaves the island with a good feeling, even in her gut.

"I'd love a glass of rosé," Melinda says to Quinn.

"Usual, you two?" asks Quinn, and we both nod. I'm exhausted. The day took a lot of mental energy, and I feel the weight of Tippy's hopes and dreams tied up into all of this. Being on for this many hours takes work.

"So, I shared the history of pickleball, but let me also tell you a little about the rest of our island lore. Dave's parents own a store, Cedar & Fern..."

I sit back and turn my ears off while Tippy waxes on about the most mundane facts of Greensea. I'm thankful when Quinn plays "Closing Time," signaling the last call for the bar.

"What's the timeframe for the decision by the network, Melinda?" Tippy asks before taking the last sip of her vodka.

"Our other producer is at the other location. We'll get back and compare notes. We want to move quickly. Film in the summer and have it out for November sweeps, so I'm sure you'll hear something pretty soon."

Tippy nods her head. The confidence she had while we were on the pickleball court has dissipated. We finish dinner and head down to the ferry for the 10:05 departure but when we pull up to the terminal it's empty. Like no cars dropping off passengers. And there's no ferry waiting to dock. There's a ferry pulling out into the harbor. Must've just missed it. Tippy walks into the terminal to check with a ferry worker.

"Minor emergency," she says, and she gets back into the car. "Looks like there's not another boat until six AM. The Olympia broke a rutter, and the Shelton has to go in for maintenance after its last run."

I look at Tippy and her eyes are screaming, "Holy crap. What are we going to do?"

"Does stuff like this happen often?"

Tippy looks at me, confused, worried, maybe even a bit mad. Although it's her fault—if she hadn't kept talking and trying to sell Greensea with her long-winded history of the island and everyone on it, we would have made the last boat.

"I wouldn't say often." Tippy scrambles. "Ferry issues are avoidable. This is my fault. I should have checked the time and stopped jabbering long ago. This is a nonissue in the summer."

Now Tippy's lying through her teeth. Ferry issues are a major problem. Not enough crew, old boats, emergencies. You name it, it happens to our ferries.

"The Greensea Inn might have a room," I offer.

"Dave, we can't put our guest up in a hotel!"

I'm afraid to know what Tippy's going to say next, but it'd better not be to offer the house we're fake living in.

"You'll stay at Meadowcroft, of course."

I turn around and glare at her. She hasn't thought it through.

"That sounds lovely! Thank you, Tippy! Any chance I can borrow some things from you? I brought nothing for overnight."

"Absolutely. Let's head to the house, Dave."

The lasers I'm shooting through the rear-view mirror seem to miss Tippy. I drive faster than I should back to Meadowcroft, hoping Bob doesn't give me a ticket but wishing the earth might swallow me whole.

"I have plenty of space for you. It will be a sleepover."

Where's Tippy planning on putting me? In the doghouse? At her parents'? She can't do that, because Melinda thinks we live together, which implies we live in the same room.

"That's so sweet of you two!" she says.

"You can have my room, and I'll stay on the couch," Tippy offers.

"What about Dave?" she asks.

Bingo. Thanks, Melinda. Yeah, what about me?

"Do you have a guest room?" asks Melinda.

"Oh, yeah. Sorry! Wasn't thinking." Tippy opens a water bottle and takes a long swig.

"We just had it painted," I add, saving her butt. "Tippy keeps forgetting that it's ready to be used again."

Cha-ching. Me to the rescue again. And I'm about to be stuffed into Tippy's walk-in closet so we can keep up this little charade. I pull in the driveway, dreading what's ahead.

"Oh, look!" says Tippy as we're all getting out of the car. "A deer!"

She motions to Melinda to come toward her. Melinda does, and as if Tippy and I are on the same wavelength—which is scary to imagine—I run into the house. Bear barks and I shush him. I grab all of my crap out of the guest room and the bathroom and throw it on Tippy's bed. I'm glad I at least made the bed this morning before I left. An old habit from my younger days that's never quite left me, thankfully. I walk out of the room just as I hear Tippy talking in a loud and exaggerated way.

"Well, I guess it wasn't a deer. Silly me!" She looks around and catches me standing in her doorway. I give her a quick nod.

"How about a glass of wine, and we can sit on the patio next to the fire pit?" Tippy asks.

"I'm exhausted," says Melinda.

Fine by me. I'm peopled out.

"Oh, I'm sure you are. Let me grab some things for you."

Tippy disappears into her room.

"Can I get you anything? Water? Tea?" I don't know what else Tippy has or where to find anything else, so I hope one of those suffices.

"A glass of water would be nice," she answers, looking around the family room.

At least I know where the glasses are, and the water faucet. Tippy comes back out with a pile of things before Melinda realizes I'm not a part of any of the possessions in the entire house.

"A clean set of pajamas for you! The bathroom has packages of new toothbrushes, toothpaste, and makeup wipes. Stocked with pretty much all the essentials."

"Wow, Tippy! Pretty impressive," says Melinda. "Hostess with the mostest, even on a moment's notice."

"She learned it from her mom," I say. "Bell is legendary. Everyone always wants an invitation to one of her parties!"

Melinda takes the pajamas and her glass of water, and Tippy shows her to the guest room. I can hear Tippy showing her where everything is, and a sense of panic comes over me as I realize we're about to spend the night feet from each other. The rush of hiding the fact that I'm sleeping in the guest room and not with Tippy distracted me from the fact that we're about to sleep in the same room. How many preschool lullabies will I have to sing to lull myself to sleep tonight?

Tippy comes back out of the guest room and motions to me to follow her into her room. She closes the door and starts whisper-yelling.

"What are we supposed to do?" she asks.

"Seems pretty obvious to me. We sleep in here," I say, pointing to the room.

"Yeah, but there's only one bed! This is the worst nightmare of all romance novels. It's the moment that changes everything. You've seen it in the movies time and time again."

"Calm down. I'll sleep on the floor in the corner, and you take the bed."

I run my feet over the floor. Soft enough. Good padding under the rug. Tippy walks into her bathroom and comes out with a couple more blankets.

"You sleep in clothes, right?" She throws the blankets on the floor.

"Not like a pair of jeans. Just boxers."

"Tonight it's head-to-toe clothes for you, buddy." She points up and down my body.

I brush my teeth and make myself comfortable on the floor. Tippy takes what feels like a year and a half in the bathroom. With the faint smell of herbs trailing behind her, she walks out and settles into her bed with Bear at her side.

I wiggle around in the blankets trying to figure out what position will be the most comfortable on the floor—back or side. Side wins and I stick a pillow under my hip.

"You know, your house looks nothing like I expected," I say from the floor making an attempt to ease the tension.

"What'd you expect?" Tippy asks from her bed.

"You know how you wear white a lot?"

She mumbles an "mmhmm." "I thought it would be modern and crisp. All white save a few metal pieces, just like your clothes."

But Tippy's room is painted navy. She has a brass headboard and a thousand throw pillows on her bed. My mom would love it. Florals. Polka dots. Stripes. They all match somehow. Some of the same blues run through each pillow. Her comforter looks inviting, all white and thick, like a cloud landed in the middle of her room. Each side of the bed has a nightstand with dainty lamps and books.

"Yeah, modern isn't all my vibe. I like a bit of a hodge podge in my house."

Tippy turns on the TV, another thing I didn't think I'd find in her room. She chooses *Jaws* from the long menu of choices.

"Interesting pick."

"Top five favorite movie of all time," she says and that tracks that she'd like a movie about sharks eating humans.

Bear stands up on the bed and growls toward the door. A second later there's a gentle knock. Tippy and I both look at each other. If Melinda sees me on the floor, our charade is over. She scoots over to the right, and I leap up and get under the covers. I stick my foot out and kick my bedding into a pile so it doesn't look so set up. She may not see it from the door anyway.

"Yeeees," says Tippy.

The door opens a crack and Melinda peeks in. "I'm so sorry to bother you two. I just realized I don't have a phone charger. Any chance you have an extra?"

Tippy slides out of bed in her little cream pajamas. "Sure!" She walks toward the door and closes it behind her.

Can't get back on the floor now. What if Melinda comes back? I get up, make a neat pile of my bedding, and get back in bed. Tippy walks in and stands behind the closed door.

"That was too close for comfort," she says. "You're a pretty good leaper."

I surprised myself with my ability to levitate into the bed so quickly and easily.

"Let's take these pillows and make a wall down the middle. I promise I won't cross the line." It's a trick we used to do when we were staying in hotels together on family vacations. Someone always had to share a bed with Jac, and we made a wall of pillows so we didn't catch cooties.

"Don't you think we're mature enough to not need any pillows? Just keep your body parts on your side, and I'll keep mine on my side. We should be fine!" Tippy snorts.

"We can handle that, but what if an arm comes flying over to my side in the middle of the night?"

"Push it back," she says.

"Random leg kicks me?" I ask.

"Kick it back."

Hopefully the subconscious, sleepy part of me doesn't remember what Tippy looked like with the oyster. Or when her robe slipped down. As long as that's the case, we shouldn't have any problems.

"I don't flail in my sleep. I'm a silent and calm sleeper. And anyway, Bear will be right between us."

I look right into his little black eyes. Perfect. I love furry animals just as much as my bivalves, but this one is hogging the pillow.

"I'm not tired yet." My adrenaline is still pumping through my veins, and I don't expect it to calm down soon.

"Want to keep watching the movie?" Tippy asks.

"Sure."

The room gets quiet with echoes of the iconic music. When Tippy doesn't move for ten minutes, I'm pretty certain she's asleep. I roll over and try to do the same, but I can't stop thinking about today. Yeah, it wore me out, but being with Tippy and impressing her with my pickleball knowledge filled me up more than I expected and I realize I'm losing the desire to poke the bear.

―――

The movie's off when I wake up, and a tail wags in my face. It's two AM, and I look over at Tippy, sound asleep. Little tendrils of curls frame her cheeks as she sleeps on her side, facing me. Her eyes are covered with a sleep mask. I feel the warmth of her breath. Bear's tiny snore. I'm calm here, and I don't understand it. I usually can't deal when I'm away from the water. But Tippy's room smells like lavender or something. Not perfume-y, just soft and relaxing, and it makes me miss the sound of the waves less.

———

I slip out of bed while Tippy's still asleep to take Melinda to the ferry. She sits up when I get out of the bathroom.

"I'll be out in a minute," she says with an enormous yawn. "Haven't slept that well in a long time."

Tippy hugs Melinda at the door. And Melinda looks at both of us. Like she's waiting for something. Expecting something.

Tippy's standing there in her short-short pajamas with her hair in a messy red bun. And I can't resist. I put my hand on the side of her face and lean in. Her lips are soft and welcoming. This should be just a little peck, but I want to run my tongue along her teeth. Grab her hair and let it out of the scrunchie. And then push her against the wall. But I don't. I pull away and say, "Have a good day."

CHAPTER TWENTY ONE

TIPPY

I fall against the door as soon as it closes.

"Holy hell! What was that?" I say to Bear, and he barks in return. I use every muscle in my core to pull myself up (Martha would be proud) and crawl back into bed, after the best night's sleep I've had in ages, to contemplate what just happened.

When his lips touched mine, it was like the finale of a Fourth of July fireworks show right in the pit of my stomach. It's like all the animosity we've had toward each other was channeled into that kiss and lit my insides on fire. Stop the presses! Hold the phone! Dave Sherman's lips set me ablaze. And it was all an act. I shake my head and pull my sleep mask over my eyes as memories of his calloused hand on the side of my face, holding me with just enough force, dance through my mind.

He did it all for show. For Melinda. Even the cute story about falling for me. Not real. We're still Dave and Tippy, archenemies. Right? This is what he was supposed to do per our agreement.

Then what's this ache in my chest? Heartburn. I must have

eaten something at The Old Owl, because this cannot be actual feelings. Right? Serves me right, playing with fire like this. Spending so much one-on-one time with someone was bound to mess with my head.

His rhythmic breathing lulled me back into the most peaceful sleep last night. The best part was, he didn't even snore. Not that that even matters. As soon as this business with the show is over, he'll win his Academy Award for acting and be gone, and I'll be back to square one with an empty bedroom, searching for my one true love.

Bear jumps into bed with me. I close my eyes and go back to sleep.

———

The sun hits me, and I open my eyes with a start.

"What time is it?"

Bear jumps up. I roll over and pick up my phone. Nine thirty! Nine thirty! I never sleep this late. I missed my Pilates class, and I'll still have to pay for it. And I missed catching all the dirt on the way to class. Now even GG won't be up to date.

I scan my brain and think about things I can do to gather info for the column.

"Let's go for a walk," I say to Bear, and then text Sylviane and ask her to meet me at Sunset Tower Park.

Twenty minutes later, Bear and I pull up on the bike as Sylviane gets out of Old Blue.

"Thanks for coming," I say.

"I needed a break from writing," Sylviane says. I get it. Writing can be a lonely task.

I lock my bike up and we walk on the path. The trail around the park takes us around the pickleball courts. They're packed with people, and I'm sure I know ninety percent of them, and I probably need to write about some of them in the column, so I take a quick glance. Betty Reynolds is playing with Debbie Smith and not her usual foursome. Tom Rickshaw is wearing a knee brace. And Laura Prescott is wearing a navy top with a black skirt. Ladies' Night at Wine Down must've been a doozy. And as she's playing pickleball, I guess my reformer would have been free at Pilates.

"Whoa, racehorse! What's got you trying to break the land speed record?" asks Sylviane.

All my energy and angst is pushing me to go at a rather fast pace. I realize I'm dragging Bear behind me, so I pick him up while we go.

"He kissed me," I say.

"Who kissed you?" she asks.

"Dave!"

"Oh, well you are fake dating, so that makes sense."

I kick a rock out of my way on the path. "You don't even care! You say that like it doesn't even matter."

"Well, does it matter?"

The question is so insane that I almost trip over a tree root.

"How can someone kissing me not matter?"

"You're 'dating.' It's all part of the act. It only matters if you have feelings for the person. If the person means nothing to you, then it doesn't matter." Sylviane picks an errant flower bud off the trail and smells it.

"I can think of a bunch of situations where that's not true."

We're near the pond, where a smattering of toddlers with their parents are looking at the baby ducks.

"Okay. Well, were you forced into anything?" Sylviane stops for a second to look at the ducklings, but Bear yips and scares them all away.

"Surprised, yes. Forced, no."

"Was it a situation where there was any sexual harassment?"

"You know the answer to that question."

"You're the one who suggested there were other situations. But in this case, you and Dave agreed that kissing fell well within the boundaries you established. So I'm trying to figure out why this situation has put so much pep in your step." Sylviane smiles.

It's true. Dave's kiss got me going more than a twenty-ounce espresso.

"He's just such a good actor." I mean, he was an amazing Will Parker in the Greensea High production of *Oklahoma* back in the day, but this is next level. He's almost got me convinced he wanted to kiss me.

My phone buzzes. I pass Bear to Sylviane and grab it out of my fanny pack.

> Dave: Sorry about this morning. Hope you're not mad.

I read it out loud.

"How am I supposed to answer?"

"Are you mad?"

This is so easy for her. Why is it so black and white? She doesn't see the conflict that's brewing in my mind.

"I'm not mad. But I don't know if I'm happy."

"Text him back and tell him. You can say that. Then see how it goes when he gets home." Sylviane laughs. "I still can't believe you two are living together."

I do what she suggests and text Dave, then take Bear back.

We're near the water tower now, and I give it a quick once-over to see if I notice any new graffiti I can write about in GG.

"What's caught your eye?" Sylviane asks.

"Oh, just the water tower."

"Have Dave's environmental ways rubbed off on you?"

"Ha! He wishes! No, I just like to check out all the graffiti. Teenagers always sneak up there and paint couples' initials. It's kind of sweet and romantic, albeit a little dangerous."

"Aww...I love an illegal romantic gesture." Sylviane reads some signs posted on the bulletin board near the water tower. "Spring Kick-Off Concert? What's that?"

"Greensea's concert series, of course! Local cover bands playing "Sweet Caroline" and other hits everyone can sing along to. People bring picnics and wine and spread out in the grass. Kids run around playing catch. It's Greensea at its best."

"We have to go to it!" Sylviane looks like I just gave her an all-expenses-paid trip to Hawaii. "Imagine if Johnny Nickel would play! *Love at the Last Resort* would love it! Speaking of, how'd the day with the producer go?"

I give her the highlights of our day.

"What're the next steps?" she asks.

"Melinda said they'd get back to us soon with a decision. She said she's going to send a list of more specific questions."

"That has to be good, doesn't it?"

We slow down to a more reasonable pace, so I put Bear down.

"Yeah, I think it's good. I mean, save the sea sickness, almost gluten poisoning, loose goat, and canceled ferry, it went well." I roll my eyes.

"What was it like spending the night with Dave? You haven't even mentioned that."

"Well, the kiss superseded all of that. But it was fine. Happy to report he doesn't snore or toss and turn."

"That will matter a lot when you two give up this 'charade.'" Sylviane uses air quotes around charade and laughs.

"What do you mean?"

"I mean, who cares if he snores? It's not like you're going to get married or anything." She gives me a wink.

Sylviane's right. It doesn't matter. After the show ends, we'll go our separate ways. He'll quit the charade. Mayor Nickerbottom will be upset at first. He'll have his told-you-so moment that will annoy me to no end. But that'll be it.

"I know," I say and pick up the pace again, changing the subject and watching the courts as we pass them for a second time. "Those people don't know how to serve."

I hate watching the ineptitude of the newbies on the pickleball court. It's embarrassing to the sport. And one of the reasons I'm teaching lessons. The popularity of the sport is mind-boggling. How could something from our little island turn into that? I dare say, Greensea is not doing a good job capitalizing on it. We should have a huge tournament here. Bring the people to us. Just another project that needs me at the helm.

My mind turns. If *Love at the Last Resort* doesn't pan out, we could do something like that. A pickleball retreat. A pickleball university. Olympics! The possibilities are endless. My fatal flaw is the plethora of ideas always running through my brain.

"What are you up to the rest of the day?" asks Sylviane.

"Figuring out my life and overthinking Dave's acting abilities, and then trying to avoid my roommate at all costs."

"Sounds healthy."

CHAPTER TWENTY TWO

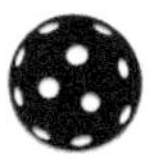

DAVE

I check on all my oyster beds. Harvest what I need and sell to my regulars. Then I grab some apple cider vinegar and wipe the shack from top to bottom. But my mind goes back to this morning. So I hike up to Hilltop in the Grand Green Forest, not allowing myself to stop until I get to the top, and then I turn around and hike back home to Bungalow Bay. My breath is hitched, but my brain remembers her soft cheek. I take a dip in the too-cold bay, still dressed in my hiking clothes, and then two hot showers. And no matter what I do, I still can't stop thinking about that kiss, because it made me wish I had been kissing Tippy for all these years instead of teasing her.

Her text said she wasn't mad, but she wasn't happy. What does that even mean? Kisses were part of our agreement, so obviously she's not mad. But did she feel anything? A modicum of pleasure? Anything? She hasn't had to undertake any extreme measures to erase it from her memory like I have.

I call Josh. He'll know what I should do.

"Yo."

"Hi, Dave. How are you?" he answers, sounding odd and professional.

"I need to talk to you."

"So badly that you've forgotten basic pleasantries?" Josh laughs. "This have anything to do with your lips?"

"What?! Has GG already posted about it? How in the hell did they find out so quickly?"

God damn gossip column! Ruins everything good on this island.

"No! Tippy and Sylviane met for a walk. I guess Tippy was losing her mind because you kissed her."

Ahh, she *is* thinking about it. Exhale.

"Losing her mind how? In a good way, or in the sheriff-is-coming-to-press-charges way?"

I throw myself down on my couch and cover my eyes. I'm not sure I want to hear his answer.

"Sylviane and I talked about it, and we think it's better for us not to get involved, any more than we already are, in whatever it is you two have going on."

What the hell?

"Wait a second! You're related to me. I understand why you might not side with Tippy, but I'm your blood relative. You're obligated to give me advice and information."

"Nope. Not going to happen." He stops and I hear him take a deep breath. "I want to keep my relationship intact, and I don't know what kind of crazy shit you and Tippy will come up with next. For my sanity, I'm staying out of all of it."

"You know what they say, 'Bros before...'"

"Don't finish that statement, Dave."

Fine. If he won't offer any advice, I need to take the bull by the horns and face my destiny at Tippy's on my own.

On the drive over to Meadowcroft, I see a bike with a sign that says "free" sitting on the side of the road next to a mailbox. I pull over and look.

Hmm...Wheels turn. Chain is in good enough condition. The handlebars could use some tape, and the seat is a little torn up. But otherwise, it looks decent. Maybe Tippy and I can even go for a bike ride together. I throw it in the back of the truck and continue on my way. I'll get it all cleaned up and looking good as new. It's obviously a sign from the fake dating gods pushing me to spend more time with her.

Tippy's car is in the driveway but it's quiet when I open the front door to her house.

"Tip?" I call. My left eyebrow twitches. I'm not sure what to say to her about this morning.

Bear comes running and barking his little yippee bark. I thought he would have been used to me by now. Especially after I spent last night in the same room as him. I pick him up and he nuzzles his head into my neck. Maybe his yip is just his way of saying hello.

Tippy's at the kitchen table. Headphones on. Hair up in a messy bun, pencil in her mouth, staring at her laptop. I set Bear down, and he runs over to her, causing her to look up.

"Working on stuff for the show." She looks back down. Doesn't take her headphones off or anything. Hint taken. I'll leave her alone.

Bear and I head outside. I get the bike out of my truck and grab my crate of tools too, in case the bike needs anything tightened. The first layer of dirt comes off with water and a rag. Bear's my buddy now, sitting next to me while I work.

I love this time of day. The sun is sinking and twilight's

approaching. Animals are coming out for dinner. It's peaceful up here at Meadowcroft. No water view, obviously. In fact, can't see much more than the tops of trees. But there's a certain quiet Zen about it all.

Bear chases ants on the ground. Carnivore, obviously. The birds start chirping in rapid succession. A murder of crows goes crazy. I hear the soft flute of an eagle. And I look up just in time to see it dive down and realize it's coming straight for Bear.

"Shit!" I scream, and turn over the box of tools and throw it over Bear. And then I throw myself over the box for extra protection. I don't move for a second.

"Nothing to see here, eagle!"

But when I look up, I see him still circling. I stand up. Bear's secure under the box but yipping like a madman. I grab the hose and start spraying it straight up in the air.

"Get back, you monster!"

I'm spraying and jumping. Bear keeps barking. And the eagle finally flies away. Just as Tippy walks outside.

"What the hell are you doing? Is that..." She takes a step closer. Her eyes pop out of her head. "Is that Bear in a box?"

She gets down on her knees. "Why is my dog in here?" She lifts it up and takes Bear into her arms. "I can't believe you'd smother him up like that!"

I'm trying to catch my breath. I point up. And then down. "Eagle. Bear. Box."

She's stroking Bear's head. "I thought you were trying to prove you weren't a caveman."

I bend down and put my hands on my knees.

"The eagle was trying to get your dog, so I dumped the box of tools and threw it over him and then jumped on top of that. Then I grabbed the hose and danced around until the eagle left."

Tippy's brow furrows. "You did that for Bear?"

"Of course." Staring at her lips reminds me of our kiss and if I wasn't out of breath I might grab her and do it again. "We're buds now. He was helping me clean up this old thing."

"That was my next question. What's this hunk of garbage doing at my house?" She points to the bike with the hand that isn't holding on to Bear for dear life.

"It's not a hunk of garbage. It's a perfectly good bicycle that I could take out with you." I pick it up and spin the front wheel.

"Take out with me?"

"Yeah. Saw it on the side of the road with a free sign and thought it might be fun as we fake date our way around the island. Could be good for appearances if we're seen together on these things."

"Appearances. Hmm." Tippy rubs Bear's head and doesn't make any eye contact with me. "You know mine's electric and yours isn't?"

"Yeah, I know. It's better than nothing though." People don't give away e-bikes.

"Barely." Tippy takes Bear and walks inside.

The kiss is hanging over us, and I want to clear the air, so I clean up my mess and head inside. But Tippy's door is closed. Another hint taken. She doesn't even want to talk to me. I have it on good authority my kisses are not that bad. No one has ever complained before, so I know she's not just disgusted by my lips. It must be the idea of me.

An hour later, I hear something at my door. A little scratch. Surely Tippy wouldn't be scratching. I crack the door and Bear runs in and jumps at the skirt on the bed. I plop him on top of the comforter and sit back and get comfy. Bear scoots over so his butt's right by my head.

Two minutes later, I hear Tippy. "Bear! Bear!"

Bear cries on the pillow.

"He's in here."

"You decent?" Tippy peeks her head in, not waiting for me to answer even though the answer is yes, I'm decent, as long as decent includes just having a pair of athletic shorts on.

"Bear! Why are you in here with him? Come here."

Tippy stands in the doorway, waiting for Bear to come. He doesn't move. Even cries a little, scooting in closer to me and licking my mouth.

"At least he likes my kisses," I say.

Tippy's face twists, and I wish I had a picture dictionary to know what it means.

"Dude, I'm just kidding! Want to talk about the elephant in the room?" I tread carefully.

"You mean your wayward lips?" She plops down on the side of the bed.

"I was just keeping up appearances. If we were really dating, we would have kissed each other goodbye in the morning. Did I take advantage? Cross the line? It's what we agreed upon when we set the rules up at the beginning, isn't it?" Words are just spilling out of my mouth at this point.

"No. You didn't cross any line. It just caught me by surprise, and I, Tippy Meadowcroft, dislike surprises."

So it wasn't the kiss, it was that she didn't know it was coming. My shoulders relax, I can work with that.

"If you'd known it was coming, you would have been fine with it?"

She shrugs. "It's not that I wasn't fine with it." She throws herself back on the bed. Her head's inches from my side. Leaning down and smothering her with kisses is all I can think about. "I just want this to work so badly."

"You want what to work?" I'm hoping there's a slight chance she means our dating scheme.

"The show, dummy."

"It will. Has Tippy Meadowcroft ever failed at anything?"

"I got kicked off the drumline in high school."

"Did you play the drums?" I know the answer to the question already. Tippy did not play the drums.

She covers her eyes with her hands. "No! But I was willing to learn! This has to be my drumline redemption." She's smiling now.

"Don't be so hard on yourself." My hand moves her hair that's spread out like a halo around her and tickling my leg.

"Why on earth did Bell and Topper even let me try out?" She's laughing and her eyes have a twinkle in them. I sing my oyster song in my head to resist the urges circling around in my brain.

"Does anyone ever say no to Tippy Meadowcroft?"

"Am I that scary?" Her eyes catch mine.

"You're a strong person, but you're more of a sour lemon hard candy with a sweet and chewy fruit center."

"You have a way with words, Dave Sherman." She looks away. "Ugggghhhhhh. Is that why you've been mean to me for so long?"

"Mean to you? Some good ribbing and light teasing isn't being mean to you." I twist one of her hairs around my finger.

"I had to bribe you to spend time with me so we can 'pretend' we're a couple."

That's true, but if I'm being honest with myself right now, I wouldn't mind hanging out with her even if we weren't fake dating. For the second night in a row we're in bed together, and I'm not sure how to handle it. I want to touch more than her hair after this morning's kiss.

"Tip?"

"Yes?"

"Why are you in bed with me?"

She jumps up, pulls her hair away from me, and grabs Bear,

who whines like a spoiled little child, but before she leaves the room I tell her, "And Bear just wants to cuddle up with me because I had bacon for dinner."

Her feet keep on moving, but I know she heard me. I close my eyes and try to will her to come back.

CHAPTER TWENTY THREE

This time there's no way Bear's sneaking out of my room. I close the door and throw a few pillows in front of it so he won't scratch to cuddle up with Mr. Bacon again.

"I get the appeal, Bear."

Did that kiss flip a switch this morning? Or maybe it's been happening and I didn't realize it. Being near Dave seems to have eroded the feud and changed it into something more. At least on my part. I threw myself across his bed without a second thought, giving him the perfect chance to follow up this morning's kiss. Instead, he just talked about keeping up appearances and couldn't resist tugging on my hair.

I'm assuming he's not dating anyone—and if he is, he's in an open relationship—because he's never even mentioned her as a reason to not continue with our plan. Scrolling through Instagram, I find his profile. Not a lot of posts, but most of his pictures are with his high school crew. Or of his oysters. Lots of pictures of oysters shucked open. Gosh, he loves those things. There's a pic with all of his siblings. I'm friends with all of them on social media, but it means nothing. I'm friends with most of the island, even people I don't know. I click around. Nothing I didn't know. A notification pops up, letting me know someone's going Live. Glancing up, I see it's Barb, Dave's mom. What's she doing on Instagram Live? I join. Barb's standing in her kitchen. Someone's holding the phone, following her around as she gets ingredients and baking dishes out. Looks like she's making a chocolate cake and sipping from a bottle of something. Sherry?

Ha! She's laughing. Melting chocolate. Powdered sugar or flour covers the kitchen counter. People are commenting on her Live. The number of viewers keeps ticking up. A couple of names I recognize pop into the comments. Now she has the hiccups! Tom's handing her a cup of water.

"Drink that quickly," he says. She slams it and hiccups again.

I open up the GG app and start writing my column. Barb's adorable. If people aren't watching this, they need to.

Islanders,

Have you seen the new local cooking show on Instagram? Looks like Barb Sherman is trying to relive her time in Europe. She's become an overnight Instagram star, recreating foods she had on vacation. Her first try was a chocolate cake with a sherry drizzle she had in Switzerland. Give it a look...you won't be disappointed.

We vote she makes it a regular and calls it Cooking with Sherry! Why you ask, other than the fact that her name is SHERman? Watch the latest episode and you'll find out. She does a little more than cook with the sherry. Hope the hiccups have gone away. And we're all dying to know how the cake turned out!

XOXO,

GG

———

My alarm goes off at six, per usual, waking me up from a dream about eating Barb's cake. I didn't hear Dave leave this morning. He's gotten quiet in the kitchen.

Instagram and TikTok are all abuzz about the video. I'm glad I jumped on it and printed it in GG right away. Being the first to print something is one of my favorite parts of writing GG. No need to wait for any sources or anything, since it's all gossip.

The regular characters are out on my way to church, I mean Pilates. Nothing seems very gossip worthy yet. That could all change in an instant though, just like it did last night.

My regular reformer is waiting for me at The Reformation and I've thrown out my gum like a model student. The day is off to a brilliant start.

Martha starts class and my mind relaxes with the echo of her voice. It's almost as if she's a cantor at mass, singing, "push in, and push out" through the eaves of the old church. To top it all off, the sun blasts through the cross right over the altar. A truly religious experience and a harbinger of what this day will be like.

After class, I bike down to Main Street to lead the Fit Gree-nies on our weekly walk. Today we're walking around Grays

Bay. An easy route, so I plan to step up the routine as we move along.

Almost everyone's here. Marlene is stretching her quads. Shirley is reaching down to her toes. Al is putting on his ankle weights.

"Okay, Greenies! Let's get this show on the road!" I grab my visor out of Bertha's basket, and we start with a gentle walk. Four minutes in, we change to high knees. Fit Greenies is another opportunity for me to be out and about, getting some info for the column and a chance to make some extra money. These people pay me well to lead them around the island even though they could do it on their own.

"So Tippy, tell us all about the day with the producers!" Marlene, the group busybody, asks.

Shirley picks up her pace and leans in to hear more as I recount our day.

Al butts in at the end. "Now, Tippy, you have said 'and then Dave' six times. I was skeptical about the two of you when you stood up there at that meeting, but the writing is on the wall. You are in love."

They all giggle. I blow my whistle and start skipping. They'll be too out of breath to talk anymore.

———

The door slams and Dave walks in.

"When I find out who GG is, I will make sure they never type another word. I'll have them exiled from the island. Exploiting my mother like that. How could they?"

Shit. I didn't mean to make him mad. The damn video went viral. I'm not the only person who said something. How about all those Instagrammers? But she was cute! And that's what I focused on.

"I didn't think what GG said was that bad." I put down my blue-light glasses and stop working on the admin tasks for the *Gazette*.

"They're taking advantage of my mom for their own personal gain." Dave pours himself a cup of coffee.

"But other people did that too?"

"I don't know the other people."

"You don't know GG either."

His eyes feel like lasers searing into my soul. I cross my toes and all my fingers, hoping the lie will wipe over me.

"You know what I mean!" He scowls.

I know what he means, and his anger's worrying me. What will he do if he finds out it's me? He's going to hate me. This whole charade will fall to pieces. I can't let him know.

"I think it's cute that your mom is an influencer." I'm afraid to tell him the stats on the GG post were higher than usual.

"She's not an influencer. She's just doing a little cooking show. It's not her fault she didn't realize how much alcohol that sherry had when she was doing a Live. I can't believe she even knows what a Live is."

Barb's red cheeks were adorable. Her giggles are a meme.

"I'm sure GG meant nothing by it." I pick up my glasses and bite on the end of them.

"It's time for GG to stop. We don't need a gossip column around here anymore. I think they're doing more harm than good." He paces in front of the table.

"I don't think that's true. She shares information. A lot of what she says keeps neighbors together." I look down at my laptop, trying to avoid any eye contact.

"She? You know who it is, don't you? You have to. Topper owns the damn paper."

Uh oh. Insert sock in my mouth.

"Slip of the tongue. They. He. Who knows? Dad is tight-lipped about GG. None of us knows anything about the person. As far as I know, I haven't ever seen GG." I stop and make it look like I'm thinking. "But maybe I see them every day and don't know."

"Well, when I find out who it is, they're going to get more than a bunch of spoiled oysters from me."

"You have spoiled oysters?" Changing the subject seems like a valid option.

"No. But I could leave some out in the sun for a little and see what happens."

"Diabolical Sherman."

I excuse myself and walk into my bathroom under the guise of taking a shower. He's going to be so pissed when he finds out I'm GG.

I turn the water on. Hot as it'll go. The water runs down on my hair. He'll hate me as soon as he finds out it's me. He'll quit the show. Give up on our plan. Payback will be a bitch. Leave it to me to ruin a fake relationship. I'm destined to live on my own for the rest of my life. Like a spinster locked in a turret.

What if I find someone else to take over GG and leave it behind forever? Dave doesn't have to know it's me. We can keep it a secret. But I love being GG. I've created a character and grown to love her.

After my shower, I walk down to my parents' house, sneaking out my back door so Dave doesn't see me. Topper will have some good advice. He always does.

"Dad?" I yell in their front door. My parents' home is an old stone house. Some of the interior walls are stone and some are covered with sheetrock. But it emanates safety and strength. The back of the house is all windows looking out to a large deck and hundreds of trees.

"Out here, Sweets!" Dad says from the deck. He loves to sit out there and watch the birds. You hear a little bird chirp, and

Topper knows the name. The chattiest one's a kingfisher, his favorite.

I pull out a wooden chair at the long table made out of a barn door and sit down.

"How are you doing, darling?" Topper genuinely wants to know how I'm doing. To be honest, he always wants to know how everyone's doing. Losing Don was an enormous loss in his life. They were best buds, secretly working together on GG. Dad was shocked to learn that Don had been writing cozy mysteries and hadn't told him. The fact that no one else knew made him feel a little better. Don just kept that side of himself hidden because of his own great pain about the loss of his sister, Sylviane's mom.

"I'm not okay, Dad." There's never any use lying to him. He always figures out the truth with his probing journalistic questions. Now would be no different.

Topper crosses his arms and sets them on the table. "Tell me everything."

So I do.

"I don't think you've done anything wrong here. Well, I take that back. GG has made some unsettling comments, but I think you know that and try to do better. GG isn't a mean column. It brings about community. It keeps the island together. It's part of our identity. It gives us commonality. Without it, we're a floating mass commuting on a boat. Maybe people look up and give each other a passing glance. But with GG, they know about the Jacobsons' triplets. They know Mr. Kim had bypass surgery and is recovering well. They laugh together about the random screamer. Or the antics at Wine Down. It's a good thing. Focus on that. Focus on what you do for others. Your comment about Barb wasn't out of line compared to some others you've written. Dave's just upset about the whole thing, and GG is the easiest thing to point to and try to control."

"But I think he'll be upset that I've lied to him." My nose starts running, from the cold I tell myself.

"Darling, you didn't lie. You just haven't told him the whole truth."

"You would've grounded me for that when I was a teenager."

Topper laughs. "Yes. Bell would have put you in your room for sure. But this thing with you and Dave is complicated. Do you know all the things he does for work? Like whose house he fixes up? Do you know that Leslie McDoodle asks him to change her lightbulbs just so she can see him in his jeans? You don't know everything about each other. You're not supposed to yet."

I take a deep breath. Topper's making me feel better about it. I still know Dave will freak when he finds out. But Dad's given me a little glimmer of hope. Something I didn't have before.

"Thanks, Dad."

I walk back home and find Dave asleep on the couch, Bear lying on top of him. Breathing in unison. Having another person in the house is nice. Something I could even get used to. I sneak into my room and crawl into bed. It will be okay, I tell myself.

I text Sylviane.

Tippy: Dave hates GG.

Sylviane: A lot of people hate GG.

Tippy: Really? I feel like they all love to hate her but actually can't live without her.

Sylviane: Possibly a more accurate description.
Are you going to tell him it's you?

Tippy: He'll hate me forever.

Sylviane: Why do you care? Because you don't
want him to mess anything up with the show,
or is there something more...?

I can't answer her questions right now because I have no
idea how to find the answers.

Tippy: Will you write tomorrow's column for
me? Just make it pretty and quirky, like your
books?

Sylviane: ...

Sylviane: I don't know, Tip. It's not really my
thing.

Tippy: Exactly why it could use some color
from an outsider. And you'll be giving me some
time to think about what I want to do next.

She doesn't answer for what feels like an eternity but actually only accounts for two or three minutes.

Sylviane: One time! I'll send you something in
the morning.

Tippy: I love you! You're the best friend I can
ever imagine having.

Sylviane: Sometimes I feel like I'm your only
friend.

Tippy: Well, that's quite an honor, then.

My eyes close but my head lingers on Sylviane's question... Why do I care if Dave Sherman ends up hating me?

GREENSEA GAZETTE

Dear Island Friends,

Spring is a magical time of year on the island. The daffodils are blooming. The trees are all green—well, they've never stopped being green. The sun's sitting a little higher in the sky, but the mountains are still covered in snow. You can see warmer days glistening in the sun rays that bounce off the water.

I thought I'd highlight some local businesses today. Just in case you can't get enough of Apollo's cinnamon rolls...Did you know they give all the leftovers at the end of each day to the ferry work-ers? Makes you love them even more! Codmothers has introduced a local farm-to-table program of sorts. One of the elementary schools is growing potatoes, and they try to source as many as they can from them. Who knew there were so many do-gooders in the restaurant business on Greensea?

We're all wondering who put the carousel horse on the baby traffic roundabout! Evelyn Cox reported she thought a demon clown was going to come and kill her after she passed by the horse in the dark.

XOXO,

GG

CHAPTER TWENTY FOUR

TIPPY

"Ultimately, we've decided to go with a place that feels less flannel and more bikini, preferably string."

There's a small hum in my ears. Like a hum that sounds like it might pierce my soul. Stop the presses. Hold the phone. Tippy Meadowcroft has failed.

"You mean you're not picking Greensea?"

How can this be happening? I put everything into it. And now they want nothing to do with us. My crowning moment is a failure. What do I do now? It's all done. Over. Caput. Back to the drawing board of my dreams, just because the producers can't go with my idea for a dating show on Greensea due to our lack of adequate bikini weather.

"We can bring heaters in to keep the contestants warm while they play beach volleyball. Tents over outdoor areas to keep away the rain."

"We're sorry, Tippy, it's also a vibe thing. While the Pacific Northwest is perfect for some things, it just isn't right for a sexy show. The gigantic trees are too murder-y," replies Andrew.

Murder-y? I swear on this green island I've never heard anything so ludicrous in my life.

"I assure you, there has never been a violent crime on Greensea Island."

They all laugh. "That may have been the wrong word. We want something more tropical. More palm trees, not pine trees."

"Consider it done. We can bring in palm trees and plant them all over Swifterson."

"Tippy, the one thing the other location doesn't have is you. You're the real reason we even considered this for as long as we did," says Melinda.

All the people nod in agreement.

"Melinda shared all the stories about her time on Greensea, and my goodness, that place is a hoot," says Andrew.

Melinda chimes in again, "We're sure there's something we can try on your fair island. It's a shame to keep it hidden from the rest of the world."

"Who knows? Maybe it's time for the housewives to become more outdoorsy," says Charles.

This little bit of hope is the only thing that keeps me going. I'm a complete and utter failure where this show is concerned, but there's a glimmer in the future. Something I might pin my hopes on.

"Well, thank you for considering Greensea." I have to end graciously. If my mom has taught me anything, it's that.

"It's been a pleasure, Tippy." More nods in agreement around the screen.

"Let's stay in touch," says the head honcho, Andrew.

An open door, or at least one that nobody has slammed shut—yet.

The cranks turn as I wonder how a *Real Housewives of Greensea* would go. Bell could be the matriarch of the group. I'm sure Barb could be in it too. With the success of her Live, everyone would want her to be a part of it. Then I could get Laura Prescott to be the PTO younger-generation mom. Of course, I could be in it. I mean, I'm not a wife, but isn't it just a random term for women? I think there are single women on the actual show. Maybe it just means homeowner or people about the town.

My wheels are turning, and I think I have a viable idea for another show. Maybe the people from *Love at the Last Resort* can put me in touch with the *Housewives* producers. I mean, I dedicated a lot of time to the whole thing.

I'm acting like Bear when he finishes his bone and wants another one right away.

How am I going to tell Dave the news? That'll be it. No more guy in my guest room. No more early morning wake ups. Extra cuddles for Bear. No more *Jaws*-watching companion. No one to leave me a little extra coffee. I'll tell him over dinner. I'll tell him everything.

It's cold out. One of those dreary days that requires soup. And probably one of the days that speaks to why the producers don't want to come to subtropical Greensea. Hopping on the bike to head to the grocery store is the only thing that's going to bring me sanity. I need fresh air. And I need warm and cozy food to make for dinner tonight.

"Bear, you're staying home."

I hand him a treat and he runs to his bed.

I leave my curls down, put on my helmet, and take off on Bertha. As usual, the wind through my hair feels good. Even if it's not raining, the air's moist and misty. I lock my bike up at Island Grocers and head inside.

Tim Muffins is arguing with the produce manager. Apparently, someone's stealing berries and grapes leaving the containers half empty. Mr. Muffins has installed cameras about the greens to try and catch the culprit. I could stand here next to the bananas all day and get more information than I'd ever want from the grocery store, but I'm on a mission.

"Any news about the TV show?" Mrs. Harris, my first grade teacher, finds me next to the potatoes.

Making light of it and keeping focused on my task is the best idea for the moment. "Too soon to tell!" I lie with my best smile.

"Well, Mr. Harris and I cannot wait to see all the handsome bachelors and bachelorettes!" She shivers as she walks away. Ew.

Fortunately, I only need a few more things before I use the self-checkout (to lessen the chance of talking to anyone) and get on my bike. It's the kind of day that makes me wish I had tiny windshield wipers on my cycling glasses.

I throw on my coziest cardigan at home and turn up my music. Cueing up my sad song playlist, letting myself wallow while I cook.

Peel the potatoes. Sautee the onion. The muscle memory of the soup takes over. Even though I live alone, I try to make things nice. Set the table for myself, and for the moment Dave, I guess. It's something I do, like making my bed.

While the soup's simmering, I set out all the extras in little bowls and put them on the table. I pour myself a glass of rosé and take a drink. When I turn around, I bump into something. Someone. It's Dave. Who's now wearing my glass of wine.

"You scared me," I whisper. He's so close.

His chin grazes the top of my head like it's meant to be there. I'm stuck in one place, wine glass in between us.

"Sorry," he says in a low rumble. His voice reverberates on my forehead. We're so close to each other, and neither of us tries to move. I look up and our eyes catch. He leans down and I lift my head and we're kissing. For no one else but ourselves. It doesn't feel like he's pretending. Instead, it's magic. It's years of taunting each other. It's the energy you have as you're crossing the finish line. It's wanting so much more before you realize this kiss has just changed everything. It's every ounce of stress leaving every cell of my body. His tongue coaxes me into relaxing as his fingers catch a little bit of skin above my pant line.

He looks at me. "Hey," he says, taking the wine glass from my hand and putting it on the counter.

"Hey," I say back.

"Is someone here?"

"No, it's just us," I say.

"So, you're kissing me when no one's looking."

"Umm...yeah, I guess I am. Is that okay?"

He inches closer to me. My insides feel like a tea kettle ready to whistle. Would he be doing this if he knew we didn't need to for the show? Or if he knew I was GG? If I tell him, this could all poof away like ferry dust. But when his arms reach around me, I decide now's not the moment. Things seem to be beyond *Love at the Last Resort*. Now we're working on the Tippy and Dave show.

His hands touch my back, and I feel the strength of the fingers against my skin. He rubs down to my hips, all while holding my gaze. It's like he's looking at me just the way he looks at his oysters, with precious ferocity. I reach my mouth to his and we kiss. Again. Our tongues search for the corners of each other we don't know yet. It's like turning over a stone you've seen every day for thirty years and finding the underside covered in delicate, complex barnacles.

"Is this okay?" he asks.

"Are you still acting?"

"Not at all."

"Then it's more than okay," I whisper. I take his hand and walk him to my bedroom, closing the door so Bear stays on the other side. It's Dave. The guy who put gum in my hair. And now he's holding on to my hair like his life depends on it. He takes his time looking at every part of me like we've just met. And it's everything. The moments. The steam. So much. It even sets off the fire alarm, and I realize the soup is still on the stove.

We look at each other and laugh.

"Never set off the smoke detector before," he says. "Guess that means this was pretty hot stuff!"

I roll my eyes. "We did just go from zero to sixty in no time."

"Not really. Every interaction we've had over the last thirty years has led to this. I'd say that was a pretty slow roll."

I smile the kind of smile that makes me warm down to my toes and get up, grabbing the sheet to wrap around me.

I turn off the soup. I wrap the sheet like a toga I used to make in college and pour the soup into bowls, adding all the toppings, and carry them into the bedroom.

"Is this what you had in mind when you started making this today?" he asks.

"Not at all. Was just looking for something comforting."

"Comforting? Why?"

I take a deep breath, but I'm not ready to tell him. "Oh, I don't know. The weather? Unending dark? Uncertainty about the future? You know...the usual."

"Well, I hope this helped." He smiles.

It did. I think. Maybe. Maybe this is the something good. Maybe Dave and I are together because of this show. Maybe we're the good that's coming of it all. I smile, thinking about this day. It's been the worst of times and the best of times. Can't have a rainbow without a cloud. But can we still be a thing if we're not forced together? Will he stick around when he knows the truth? I put our bowls on my bedside table, and when I turn around, Dave's still looking at me.

"I admire you."

"Me? Why?"

"You give everything your all. When you're in, you're all in.

Take pickleball, for instance. It's not enough for you to just play. You have to give lessons and start running special events. Remember in high school when you wanted to do a dance-a-thon? Not six hours, twelve hours, but twenty-four. You had to make it all night and wouldn't rest until the principal let you do it."

"That was high school. I just did it for my college acceptance."

"But now, you didn't just clean the shack up, you turned it into a destination. There are freaking appropriately themed centerpieces on the tables. And all this with the show. You're a firecracker, Tippy Meadowcroft."

I give him a little smile. Hooking up with Dave was amazing, but being seen, like actually seen, feels even better than I can describe. But there's a whole side of me he hasn't seen.

"Thanks," I whisper.

I roll over on my back and hope there's something there. I try to think back to all of Dave's girlfriends. He was never a one-night-stand guy, was he? Maybe in college, but those drunken days don't even count. Everyone has those.

"You know you can go now," I say, testing the waters.

He props his head up with his hand. "Go?"

"Yeah. There's no one here watching us."

"Do you really think I'm that kind of guy?"

"To be honest, I don't know."

"Well, I'm not."

He pulls the comforter up and is asleep in five seconds flat. I roll over and start questioning all of my recent choices. The choice to enroll Greensea as a contestant in this show. Putting it out there to the public and putting my neck on the line. It's easy to take a chance when you aren't used to failing. And now I've taken the ultimate chance and slept with Dave. What else could I mess up?

The late night scaries start to set in. This is the worst way to start off a relationship—fake or not. How can I keep all these secrets from him? As soon as he finds out, it'll be over. And everything we felt. The synergy we created between us. It will all be gone. And I'll be alone again.

He saved Bear from an eagle. Danced around the yard like an idiot. He did all the things I would want the guy I love to do. All of them. But it's Dave. Dave Sherman. And I never thought I'd have feelings about him that didn't involve a voodoo doll.

CHAPTER TWENTY FIVE

DAVE

I walk into my house. It feels small. Cramped. The sea air rushes in, and I close the windows. It's low tide, and it smells like seaweed. The bad kind. I rip my sheets off my bed, but I know that no matter how many times I wash them, they will not feel like Tippy's. To top it off, there isn't that fancy bubbly water in the fridge.

I don't know if last night was a fluke, a moment of passion, or if it was something more. On my end, I've got all the feelings. Being with Tippy is like changing the lightbulb a couple of watts. She makes the most normal things brighter. Sure, she's bossy and takes control of everything. But she makes the things I care about better. Look what she's done for the oyster shack. I have more than a burgeoning business now. She expands my horizons, and that's not a bad thing. I love the way she eats oysters. The curve of her body. The perfect way she throws a bullseye. The way she won't stand for any crap from anyone. Her eagle-eyed precision on her goals. I'm making a list of all the things I like about Tippy, and not one of them has the ulterior motive of planning her demise.

My stomach's growling and the only thing in my fridge is a pack of expired deli meat and some Swiss cheese. Wonder if Tippy'd be interested in a date tonight?

> Dave: Want to go to The Old Owl for dinner tonight?

I stare at the screen, waiting for three dots to appear, but they don't. But my phone rings and scares the bejesus out of me. Tippy.

"Hey." She's breathy and calm.

"Want to grab a bite later at The Old Owl?" Not sure how to act after a fake-date hookup.

"Hmm...What if we ride our bikes and go over to Thin Pines for dinner?"

"The club? I'm not a member there."

"I am. You can be my guest."

I haven't been to Thin Pines since Santa Brunch in high school. My parents made Josh and I keep going because Jac and Oliver were younger than us.

"Yeah. Okay. It's a date." And I regret the words the second they leave my mouth.

"A date?" Tippy's voice goes three octaves higher.

"Sure. I mean. Well, we're still fake dating because of the show. Don't we need to be seen together out in public? So, yes. A date." I shake my head about three times too many. Are we still fake dating?

"Dave..." She sounds serious, and I'm not ready for the next part. Like she's about to dump a pot of cold water on my idea.

"I'll be back at Meadowcroft around five, and we can head over."

"Yeah. Okay. We can talk at dinner."

Shoot. Talk. What does she want to talk about? She regrets last night. I know it. She's going to dump my fake-dating ass. Operation Bring on the Charm begins tonight. Tippy will not be able to resist Dapper Dave.

———

I realize it was a waste of time (and water) to shower before heading out on our bikes. This hunk of metal is not as fast as Tippy's no matter how hard I pedal. I'm exerting more than double the energy to even stay close enough so I can still see her. She stops and waits for me to catch up.

"Dude, you're going to need to try a little harder."

"Be quiet, Tip. There's no way this machine can hang with that one and you know it. You're just showing off." I lost my will to charm after the first hill.

"I'll turn my motor off."

But it doesn't matter. Tippy Meadowcroft is just in better shape than I am. I walk the bike up the last hill to the club.

Thin Pines sits up on a cliff overlooking the harbor. It got its name because there are a bunch of pine trees that resemble toothpicks on the ninth hole of the golf course that became a landmark. People try to make a shot through them, and the number of times people hit them is remarkable given how thin they are.

The club's made quite a name for itself in the region. Raising its dues. Charging members exorbitant amounts to stick around. Kind of bold, because we live on an island and there are a finite number of people who can even join the club. But from what I can remember, the best part about it is the underpriced food.

"Good evening, Ms. Meadowcroft," says a guy at the host's stand. "Regular table in the bar?"

"That'd be perfect, Arnie. Thanks."

Nothing's changed in here in the last decade. The green wall to wall carpet with gold stars probably still has a stain from the chocolate milk I spilled on it as a kid. If the dark wood walls could talk, I'm sure they'd have more to say than GG.

I pull Tippy's chair out for her since Dapper Dave has caught his breath again. Tippy looks at the menu and then sets it down. Picks it up again. Sets it down again. Then she taps her nails on it like I'm holding her up, so I set mine down too. But she keeps tapping her nails.

"You okay?"

She flattens her hand on the menu.

"What? Me? I'm fine."

She's lying; I can tell since she's not making eye contact with me. The server comes by and takes our orders.

"Any news from the producers?"

She gets that deer in headlights look and shrugs me off.

"Glad GG laid off my mom today." I change the subject.

"Did your mom do anything for GG to report on?"

"Not that I know of. She says she's going to record herself next time and then post it so she avoids anything embarrassing like that again."

"Good idea. Look, Dave..."

I don't want to discuss anything serious right now. Sitting in the middle of the bar area at Thin Pines is not where I want her to say last night was a mistake. We still have to bike home together and I'm not sure if I'll even be able to do it on a full stomach.

"Let's just enjoy our night. No need to discuss anything serious."

"You don't even know what I'm going to say."

"And I don't want to. Remember? Nothing too serious. Let's have a little fun."

The Bergnat twins run by, covered in chocolate from the free Girl Scout Thin Mints they give out in the snack area by the bar. It used to be the bane of my mom's existence when we were little. One time Oliver stuck a bunch of them in the back pocket of his dress pants, and they melted all over him and the car by the time we got home from Easter brunch.

Tippy leans away as the twins run by again. The fuzzy white sweater she's wearing wouldn't wash well if messy hands touched it.

"How many kids do you want?" I ask, as Mrs. Bergnat marches the boys out by their collars.

Tippy gets that wistful look on her face. The same one she had the other night in the pickup. "As many as I can."

"Me too," I say, even though she doesn't ask.

"Just seems like it's never going to happen."

"What do you mean?"

Technically speaking, we were pretty close to making it happen.

"Kind of stuck in this fake dating relationship right now. That puts everything on hold," she says.

My heart starts to move down to my knees. "I thought we were beyond the fake part." I raise my eyebrows.

"You did? I mean, you do? Didn't you call this a fake date when you 'asked' me out today?" Tippy asks.

"Yeah. Well, I wanted to make sure you would say yes to dinner. But we kind of crossed that fake line last night, right?"

"But it's weird." She fumbles with her napkin. I reach for her hand and hold it.

"The way we started?"

"I guess. The whole thing." Her hand's sweaty in mine. I hold it tighter to slow her quickened pulse.

"Look. There are lots of reasons people get together. Just because our way wasn't traditional doesn't mean it's wrong."

Tippy pulls her hand back. What the heck? Did I read this all wrong? Does she not want us to be together?

Thankfully our server puts our food in front of us, and we can focus on that. We eat in silence and I have a hard time figuring out how to bring on the charm as I eat my shrimp scampi.

Tippy signs for the check, and we get our reflective gear on to get ready for the dark ride back to Meadowcroft. At least it's mostly downhill this time, so I shouldn't have to get off and walk. I'm behind Tippy again as we ride home, even though she's still not using her motor.

"You just don't want to be next to me, do you?" I yell so she can hear me.

"I promise I'm not trying. When was the last time you rode a bike, Dave?"

"I don't know. Ten years ago?"

"I ride every single day. Rain or shine. Of course I'm going to be faster than you."

At her driveway she slows down to my speed, which at this point is a crawl, but I find some strength and push ahead of her.

"Not a chance, Sherman!" Tippy yells from behind, passes me, skids out, and falls over.

Shit. I jump off my hunk of metal and run over to her.

"Tippy! Don't move!"

She groans from underneath the bike.

"Just take Bertha off of me and I'll be fine."

Bertha? Her helmet?

"The bike, dummy!"

I lift the bike up, and she tries to stand up.

"Shit! That hurts."

"What hurts?" I don't want to pick her up until I know where the pain's coming from.

"My shoulder!" She looks at me, tears in her eyes. "I think I messed it up."

"Okay. I'm going to pick you up from this side and carry you to the couch." I take her helmet off first. Her hair's loose and hangs down around both her shoulders. In other circumstances, the two of us on the ground together would be romantic. But now, I look into her eyes and hope she feels safe.

She lays her left arm across her stomach like it's a broken wing, and I gently scoop her up.

"Go slow." Her breath hitches. Shit, shit, shit. She's in a lot of pain.

"I've got you. I'm just going to turn the doorknob." I press her legs against the door for a second to help balance her as I turn the knob, and then I set her down as gently as I can on the couch. I stroke my thumb over her forehead. "I'm going to call Topper and Bell. Then Doc."

Topper answers right away and says they'll be right up. Doc doesn't answer at first, but I leave a message. He's the only island doctor, and I know he'll call back shortly.

"Sweetie," says Bell as she runs to the couch. "What happened?"

"I fell off the stupid bike and hurt my shoulder. I can't really move it up and down."

My phone lights up with a call from Doc. I explain what's happened, and he assures me he'll be over in ten minutes. I've heard some people in bigger areas use the term "concierge doctor," but for us islanders, he's just our Doc and available any time we need him. He's one reason I love this place.

"Does anything hurt anywhere else?" asks Topper. "Your head? Leg?"

"No. I fell right onto my shoulder."

"Okay. Well, Doc will be here in no time, and we'll see what he suggests."

As if on cue, there's a knock on the door. Topper walks over and lets him in. Doc's known us all since we were kids. He knows our long history, so I'm not surprised when he shakes his head and smiles when he sees me.

"Still can't believe you two are a thing." And walks right over to Tippy. "Hello, Tippy. Tell me where it hurts."

Going to the same doctor at thirty-two that you saw when you were five makes you feel you're always one step away from getting a lollipop. Doc feels around Tippy's shoulder and asks her to move it, which she can't.

"Well, Tip, I think you've dislocated it. Easy fix, I'm just going to pop it right in, but it's going to hurt."

"I'm tough. I can take it."

"I know you can, but let's have Dave come over and hold you on this side." Doc has her swing her feet down to the floor and motions to me to sit next to her.

"Turn your head into Dave. Dave, you wrap your arms around here."

Doc positions them around and across her hips. It's kind of like Doc turned me into a seatbelt.

"Don't let go." Doc looks at me like he might hit my knuckles with a ruler.

Doc lifts, presses, and pushes Tippy's arm. She screams into my chest and digs her fingernails into my thigh, causing me to lift off the couch a little.

"Mother clucker, that hurt," I yell as her nails almost go through my jeans.

"That hurt? It hurt you?" I'm getting the Tippy dagger eyes.

Shoot. Not what I meant to say.

"No. No. I'm feeling your pain. Sorry. Are you okay?"

Doc wraps a sling around Tippy and grabs some pills from his bag.

"Take one of these now and switch to Advil in the morning.

I'll have Diane email you some instructions. You need to rest, and no physical activity for a few days. Then we'll look at you in the office."

Topper thanks Doc and walks him to the door. Bell makes a cup of tea for Tippy and offers to help her get ready for bed. They walk back into her room, leaving me with Topper.

"Son, thank you for all you did for our girl tonight."

I stick my hands in my pockets. "I think it's my fault. She was racing me." I look down at the floor.

"Tippy Meadowcroft has never done a thing that she didn't want to, especially for a boy. You know that better than anyone."

He's right, I do know that.

"I'm here tonight, so I'll make sure she's okay."

"Appreciate that."

Bell comes out of the bedroom, and I walk them to the door.

"She's in quite a mood. Good luck, Dave," she says, and the door closes behind them.

CHAPTER TWENTY SIX

TIPPY

Dave tiptoes into my room.

"I'm awake. No need to walk like that."

"Sorry, just trying to be quiet."

I sigh. I shouldn't be mad at him. It's not his fault, and he did all he could to help me. And it's not his fault that everything in my life is falling apart. No more Pilates. No pickleball. No driving. No biking. No getting dressed on my own. Oh! And no more show. And Dave will leave me too as soon as he finds out there's no reason to be here and that I'm GG.

"I'll sleep on the floor so I'm here if you need anything."

"You don't need to. I'll be fine."

Last thing I need is the guilt of him staring at me.

"I insist."

Mom propped me up with a dozen pillows before she left, and Doc's medicine is making me drowsy, my eyes are heavy already.

I sleep like a baby and Dave tries to be quiet when he leaves, but his rustling around wakes me up. My shoulder hurts, and I remember how much everything in my life stinks right now. I've destroyed everything around me.

Dave walks into my room with a cup of coffee, a glass of water, and a few Advil before he goes to take care of his little creatures.

"Can I get you anything else before I go?"

He's so kind, and it's literally killing me. And I want to be kind back and to kiss him before he goes. But I can't, because I'm a liar and I can't do anything else until he knows the truth, or truths. The sun's not even up, and I'm not doing it right now. I should have done it last night, or right after I found out about the show. Not saying anything's been easier, and I'm going to pay for my inaction.

"No, thanks," is all I'm able to mutter, but I manage a half-smile.

He kisses my forehead and leaves. Bear curls up next to me, nudging my good arm.

———

I hear the truck pulling down the driveway at lunchtime. At least I've made it to the couch, and with Bell's help, I'm dressed.

Dave walks in with my favorite salad from The Old Owl and puts it on the coffee table. He walks into the kitchen, grabs silverware and a sparkling water. I can't even look at him as he sits on the couch.

"Hey," he says. "What's wrong? Aside from the obvious?"

I have got to get everything off my chest. Tippy Meadow-croft is not a liar, and I don't know what's compelled me to act like this. I take a deep breath that hurts my shoulder.

"The show passed on Greensea." Starting with the show's easier than GG.

He hands me my salad and some silverware.

"You're kidding me! After all you did to show them what a perfect spot this is?"

"Yeah. They want less *Northern Exposure* and more *Baywatch*."

"Of course they do. We should have seen that coming. Sorry, Tip. Maybe something good can still come of it."

Umm...no. There's nothing good coming from anything at the moment. I toss my salad with my one good hand.

"The producers are stupid for not giving you an opportunity just because it would be hard to wear bikinis. They haven't spent enough time with Tippy Meadowcroft."

Dave rubs circles on my knee.

"Did they know what kind of shape you were in when they told you? I mean, who upsets an injured person!"

And so begins the unraveling of truths...

"Remember the other day when I was making soup?" Soup is my new euphemism.

"Um, yeah. How could I forget?"

I couldn't either because it was rainbows, blue skies, flowers on a summer morn, the first ray of sunshine after the Great Dark. It was all the things. Especially the beginning of the end.

"That's when they told me."

"You knew before we...?" He points to the bedroom.

I nod.

"Huh." He stares across the room at my bookcases. "So that's why you hooked up with me? You needed some comfort?"

"No. Not at all. They were two separate things and not a reaction."

He's quiet. Thinking about it. Now one's forever entangled with the other. But I have to rip the Band-Aid off and just tell him the rest.

"There's more."

"More?" His hands are folded in his lap now.

"Something else you don't know."

He shrugs. "There's stuff you don't know about me too. We started this all backward. It's to be expected."

He's right, but he will not care when he finds out what it is. I take a deep breath, and it hurts again—when will I learn—and spit it out. "I'm GG."

He stares at me. Doesn't blink once.

"You write the column?"

I nod.

"You outed Johnny?"

"No! No! That wasn't me. I wasn't writing it then." I stop there, not wanting to add an asterisk to the legacy of Don Hamilton.

"But you wrote about my mom a few days ago?"

I nod again. "I meant nothing by it though. It was just supposed to be sweet."

"It perpetuated the image of her as a laughingstock."

"In your eyes. The rest of the world didn't see it that way."

He stands up.

"And you said all that mean stuff about Sylviane. And Josh."

I nod again. There's no defending some things I've said. It took me a bit to find my footing.

"Does Sylviane know it's you?"

"Yes. She keeps me in check now."

"Then why didn't she say anything about what you said about my mom?"

I don't know. Probably because she thought nothing of it. I shrug my one shoulder.

"I'm not going to write GG anymore. I'll stop."

Dave walks to the door. "It doesn't matter. You're not who I thought you were. I take that back, you're exactly who I thought you were." And leaves.

I push the salad off my lap and it lands all over the floor.

Bear cleans it up for me. All I want to do is curl up into the couch and I can't, so I sit there and cry. Cry because I lost the TV show. Cry because I can't do anything. But mostly cry because I just let a guy I care about get away.

After what feels like an eternity, Mom comes over. She's carrying a bright vase of flowers and a pile of books.

"Hey, baby." She sets it all down on the coffee table and kisses the top of my head. She sits down on the couch and looks at me. "Aw, sweetie. What's wrong?"

And everything flows out of me.

"You love him, don't you?"

"I just gave you a laundry list of everything that's wrong in my life, and that's the one thing you picked?"

She rubs my leg. "Because, darling, you know the rest of the stuff you mentioned is just noise. This inane plot to fake date Dave was always just a reason to be close to him."

"What?" How could she think that? "I was forced into this situation."

"Lisbeth Meadowcroft, you could have ended it at any point. But over and over again you found reasons to keep going. And then you found reasons not to tell him the truth."

She's talking to me like she used to when she asked me if I ate my lunch or if I threw it out in the trash bin at school.

"The sooner you admit you love Dave Sherman, the sooner everything will get back on track in your life."

I throw my head back and wish I could turn back time. The only problem is, I'm not sure when I'd turn it back to.

GREENSEA GAZETTE

Islanders,

This will be happy news to only three of you: Love at the Last Resort *has decided not to film on Greensea, opting for a more tropical location with scantily clad humans. It was a valiant attempt by Tippy Meadowcroft, but alas, she had to fail at some point.*

All eyes will be on Tippy and Dave now. Were they real, or was it all for the producers? Tim at Island Grocers has a pool going. Be sure to enter. All the money will be donated to youth pickleball lessons. What more could the island possibly want? Team Tippy can meet at Wine Down to discuss the whole situation, and Team Dave will meet up at The Old Owl (of course) to discuss what actions Dave should take.

Also, if you happen to see Giselle's peacock out and about strutting her stuff, please let Giselle know where Ms. Peacock can be found and picked up. We've been alerted that her animal friends, Colonel Mustard and Professor Plum, have been missing her at the farm.

XOXO,

GG

CHAPTER TWENTY SEVEN

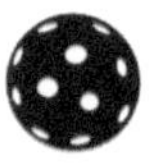

DAVE

My mind was busy whipping around just like the wind last night. I couldn't stop thinking about Tippy and GG, so I spent some time online applying for my liquor license. Imagine how great this place would be if I could serve a drink with oysters on the half shell. An old fashioned with something PNW-y in it. Of course there's only one person who would know exactly what type of drink I should make, what kind of glass it should be in, and how to adorn it. And no way, no how am I going to ask her. I can come up with something on my own, and this business will be unstoppable. TFM isn't the only one with ideas, I hope.

I head out to the shack to put out the recycled shells and check the bags. There's a bucket next to the shack for people to drop off their oyster shells so I can use them to build a reef for baby oysters. Hunter's the best at it, no surprise. I get enough to make it worthwhile but nothing that's going to change the world. I quarantine the shells and sterilize them to make sure I'm not putting diseased shells back in Bungy Bay.

Damnit. The front of the shack looks like a mini tornado

went through. The signs askew and the centerpieces are strewn across the tables. The shells that had been arranged in a perfect sculpture look like just a big pile. Pre-wind they sat crisscrossed around a candle like Mother Nature centered them on the table herself. I pick some up and try my best to make them look like something, but no matter where I place the stupid shells they don't look as nice as when Tippy did them. I shove them into the center of the table and plan to ask Mom for help.

The regulars come through all morning. Someone mentions that I shouldn't worry, they'll always be Team Dave. I have no idea what he's talking about, nor do I care. Today my focus is Sherman's Shellfish and nothing else.

But then Tippy Meadowcroft is suddenly standing in front of me in a t-shirt from a Weezer concert, a pair of gray sweatpants, and checkered vans, her hair piled on top of her head with pieces falling down all over, I channel my feelings (rage combined with a surge of desire to tuck her curls behind her ears) and continue to do my work.

"Hi."

She doesn't deserve pleasantries from me. "Thought you couldn't drive until your arm was out of a sling?"

"I can drive with one arm and my knees if I want to."

I keep washing the shells.

"I can't speak to someone who posts secrets in an anonymous gossip rag."

She sighs and stays silent.

"Why are you here?"

She steps closer to the shack. Her eyes have dark circles under them, and it's not a remnant from the black eye I gave her.

"Because I have to tell you something."

I wave my hands in a go ahead motion. I don't want to hear what she has to say, but I know her well enough to know she won't leave until she tells me why she's here.

She takes a deep breath and balls up one fist at her side and the other one in her sling. Then she closes her eyes and spits out three words. "I love you."

Heart stops beating.

She opens her eyes and continues. "I think I've always loved you. All the old people are right. I've provoked you because deep down I have feelings for you. I love the way you drive that old jalopy. I love the way your forearms feel. How your hands are rough with callouses but still so soft. I love how much you love your mom. I love the way you care for these godforsaken little creatures. If you can care so much for something that can't even speak to you, I know how much care you'll take with humans. With someone you love." She stops. I don't move. She clears her throat. "And I know you love me. Regardless of not wanting to speak to me. You feel the same way I always have. You're mad because I lied to you. But I told a small lie because I was scared. We're still getting to know each other. Even though we've known each other for almost thirty years. We don't know every little detail of the other person's life. Like where'd you go when you left the island for a week last October?"

She doesn't give me time to answer even if I wanted to.

"We're still in that fact-finding place, and I was going to tell you. But our enemies-to-lovers timeline went from zero to a hundred in no time. How was I supposed to mention it in between all the *Love at the Last Resort* stuff going on?"

I shake my head. I'm not giving her an inch. She kept it from me. It's pretty black and white. But her words simmer in my brain. She still didn't tell me about this huge part of her life because she knew I wouldn't like it. That's it. It feels so sneaky and underhanded. Why does she have to do it at all? I understand she did it to help her dad. But it seems like GG was the role of a lifetime for her. She relished the opportunity. And I can't imagine myself being with someone like that.

"I love the way you have different waders for different days. I love the way you saved Bear, even though you almost smothered him. I love the way you actually took the time to give Melinda information about Greensea, even though I know it wasn't your first inclination."

She takes another breath like she's about to pedal up a hill.

"I love the way you used to use your foot to hold the door open for me when I was walking into school behind you. I love the way you cleaned up Mr. Harris' paintbrushes in art class without being asked. Oh, and the way you protected Jac from that jackwagon Nick...flipping admirable! And now watching you, living with you, there have been so many other things to learn to love. Like the way the top of my head fits right under your chin. Or how your hand sits on the small of my back."

She looks at me, waiting for me to say anything, but my head feels like someone pulled all the tape out of the cassette. I can't rectify all that I know and all that I feel in an instant just because she's standing here in front of me waiting for an answer. So I just nod my head and look at my bucket.

Tippy stands there and waits for a response. I see the tears welling up in her eyes, but I still can't say anything. She turns around, gets in the car, and driving with one hand and two knees, leaves a trail of dust. And she's taking part of my heart with her. But Hunter pulls up before I can give it too much thought.

"Lover's quarrel?" he asks, because of course he saw Tippy bolting off.

I just roll my eyes. "How many today, Hunt?"

I occupy my mind with small talk about the oysters and the upcoming summer season. It's better this way.

CHAPTER TWENTY EIGHT

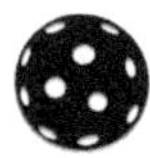

Driving isn't as easy as I made it sound. But neither is not screaming at the top of my lungs and crying my heart out. Pouring my soul out to Dave took all of my courage and I ran over my heart as I peeled away. How could he be so insensitive? His heart's frozen. Solid. Writing GG isn't even all that bad. Can't he see that I have feelings for him? Me, Tippy Meadowcroft, fell for Dave Sherman. I said I loved him and no matter how many times I glance in my rearview mirror he's not running after me.

Bear greets me at the door, at least he still loves me. I pull myself together. No more disheveled Tippy. I'll put her in the pile for Goodwill with the Weezer t-shirt. My only choice is to move ahead with Operation Forget About Dave Sherman at full speed.

I shimmy back and forth to get in my power pickleball outfit without hurting my shoulder. It's worse than playing a game of Twister but I hope it shakes me out of my mood.

Al and Shirley from the Fit Greenies are on their way

over for a blue plate special couple's pickleball lesson. I encouraged them to come later in the evening so I could test out the lights and get the full effect, but they prefer to be home before *Jeopardy* starts and who am I to argue with true love. Having my shoulder in a sling for my first couple's lesson is not ideal as I can only show them how to play using my words. No demonstrations. My skills will be tested on many levels but since the lesson is on the house, anything I offer is better than nothing.

Mom's set up her little hostess table on the side of the court for me with fresh flowers and pickle juice martinis—light on the gin so everyone stays sober. She's made pickle and pimento cheese tea sandwiches. She feels bad for me in my desperate situation—no boyfriend and a dislocated shoulder. So of course she's gone all out with the little extra touches, food served on paddles, a green and white tablecloth, it is her love language (and her business) after all. Dad even set up the ball machine for me. What would I do without them?

Since this is a beginning lesson and the whole purpose is a date, I'm going to keep them on the same side of the net. Maybe even have them position each other. Drum up the romance.

Al and Shirley pull up right on time in their sky blue Prius.

"Well dear, I don't know how you're going to teach us to play when you're in that get up." Shirley points to my sling.

"Have no fear, I'll direct you with my voice. The lesson will be more auditory than visual."

They both walk over to the court. Shirley's dressed in leggings and a tennis skirt. She's wearing a Pickleball University sweatshirt. Hmm...I'll have to make some Meadowcroft pickleball swag. My Greenies can be a (literal) walking advertisement.

Al goes right for the sandwiches and pops one in his mouth. "Nice touch, Tippy!"

I hand them each a paddle. "Okay," I walk to the baseline,

and point to where each of them will stand. "Shirley, you're here and Al, you go there."

I head to the ball machine. Shirley looks like a natural, but Al looks like he's about to tie his shoe.

"No, no! Get erect, Al!"

Shirley drops her paddle and keels over laughing. "Oh, sweetie! If only!" As she laughs my chest hurts with the flashback to my lesson with Dave.

"Al, you need to stand up, um, straighter." I change up my choice of words. "Shirley, wrap your arms around Al and show him how to stand."

Shirley giggles and walks over to Al and pulls him up a little straighter and pats him on the back.

"Stay there, Shirley. Keep your hands on Al and help him hit the ball when it comes to him."

"Oh la la," says Al and rocks his hips back and forth.

"Tippy my friend, you have a good thing going here," smiles Shirley as she guides Al to hit a ball. Take this plus a glass of wine under the lights and my pickleball lessons will be legendary.

After a few minutes, Al gets the hang of hitting the ball and we get a little rotation going between them. Every time Al passes Shirley, he hits her bottom with the paddle and Shirley giggles. If I hadn't run over my heart, it'd be cracking over and over again. I want to be Al and Shirley.

"How'd you two meet?" I can't believe I don't know after all the time I've spent with them.

"We met on the ferry. We each took the 7:05 to work every day. I always do the jigsaw puzzle and one day Al sat across the booth from me. The rest is history."

"I saw her green eyes studying those puzzle pieces and couldn't resist." Al smiles and walks over to the table.

"I love that story!" I try to fake enthusiasm, but my smile falls.

"Trouble in paradise?" Shirley asks.

"Kind of." I bend down and pick up some of the balls strewn all over the court. "I think I just need to forget about Dave."

"Every relationship has a dark moment. Not like you to give up so easily." Al takes another sandwich. "If anyone can win Dave over, it's Tippy Meadowcroft."

"You've got us old folks traipsing all over the island backwards. Dave Sherman is nothing in comparison."

Maybe they're right. Maybe today was only the beginning of trying to win him over.

Bear meets me at the door with my grandma's oyster pillow in his mouth. The thing is three times his size, and he never messes with my stuff. But he barks at me and sprawls out on top of it. My head's spinning and my shoulder throbs as I think about the oyster man who got away. But I have the beginning of a plan.

CHAPTER TWENTY NINE

I move through my day like I'm walking in cement and don't think about anything other than the task ahead of me.

Josh and Sylviane pull up late afternoon. I'm sure they've heard about Tippy's meltdown on my front lawn yesterday.

"Hey, what brings you guys by?" I ask.

"Umm...yeah. It's Dad's sixtieth birthday party, remember? We're heading over there together," Josh reminds me.

How could I have forgotten? Tippy drove off with my brain yesterday.

Josh raises his eyebrows. "A little distracted, maybe?"

"Still mad at her?" asks Sylviane, cutting right to the chase.

"Of course!" I say. "She's GG. How could I not be?"

"She doesn't do it to hurt people," says Sylviane.

"Blah blah blah. I've heard it all. But I still don't love it."

I'm a meat and potatoes guy. I don't like all this subterfuge. Keep it plain and simple for me. Maybe that's the whole problem with Tippy and me. She's not simple.

Thankfully, the drive is short.

"Happy birthday, Dad!" I give him a hug and hand him my perfect gift—noise-canceling headphones for Mom so she won't yell at him every time he chews. As the cherry on top of his birthday, his new Airstream arrived and sits in the driveway.

Jac comes running out of the silver can and gives me a huge hug.

"I missed you!" she sings. Johnny comes out behind her and gives me one of those pat-on-the-back hugs.

Mom pops her head out of the camper and yells, "Dave! It's your turn to see our new house."

I walk in and feel like I'm inside a modern apartment. Like there should be Muzak playing from the stereo. There are purple lights illuminating the ceiling. A leather couch. Sleek table and chairs. The cabinets are black with platinum hardware.

"Isn't it amazing?" Mom has her hands on her cheeks like she's just won the lottery.

"It sure is something," is all I can muster. I peek in the bathroom. Normal looking, albeit small. There's a small doorway leading to a bedroom that's mostly taken up by an enormous all-white bed. There's built-in cabinetry everywhere.

"You guys are going to fit a lifetime of stuff into this vehicle?"

"Not exactly. We'll keep some stuff on the island and only travel around with what's necessary."

They're not keeping it at my house, that's for sure. "Where? That storage unit in town?"

"We'll talk about the details soon. Let's go join everyone else."

Dad, Josh, Sylviane, Jac, Johnny, and Ollie are all on the back deck. Jac's put her elementary school teacher skills to work and decorated the deck with a balloon arch and crepe paper. Dad's wearing an apron decorated with puffy paint that Jac must've made. Ollie hands me a visor bedazzled with glitter so I can match the rest of the crew.

"Festive." I look around at all of them. They're looking at me like they have something to say, but I will not give them the satisfaction.

"So the RV's here. That means this could be our last meal together in this house?" I ask.

"Dude, it's Dad's birthday. Let's talk about something happier," says Josh.

Jac giggles and grabs Johnny's arm. They both look at Mom and Dad, and Dad gives them a little nod.

"We're going to buy the house!" Jac blurts out.

"You as in you and Johnny?" I ask.

"Sure are," answers Johnny. "We need somewhere to stay when we visit the island, and I couldn't dream of letting someone else get their hands on the place where I met your delicious sister."

They look at each other and kiss.

"Gross," I mutter under my breath and stick my finger down my throat like I'm going to vomit.

"Just because you're unhappy doesn't mean you can't be happy for the rest of us," says Jac.

"So, this is where you'll leave the rest of your stuff?" I look toward Mom.

"Yes, we're going to clear out our things and put them in the attic. Johnny and Jac have some ideas for a little remodel, and we want them to make this house into whatever they'd like, but there will be a place for us to keep everything."

"And a place for us to hook up whenever we're in town," Dad offers.

"Gross," I say in a louder voice this time, repeating the gesture.

"Hook up to the water and electricity, idiot." Ollie pats me on the back.

Dad sets a plate of burgers on the table, and we dig in. It's all our traditional family barbeque food. Potato salad, potato chips and French onion dip, baked beans, corn on the cob, and a green salad because Mom always insists.

"How's the oyster business going?" asks Ollie.

"Fine." Thinking about the shack makes me think about Tippy, and I'm not in the mood to do that.

"Where's Tippy, sweetheart?" Mom looks at me like she's reading my mind as she squirts some ketchup on her cheeseburger.

"Tippy? Why would she be here?"

"Because I thought you were living together." She takes a bite, and I wonder if she's baiting me, or if she really doesn't know what happened.

"Didn't you read the article in GG? *Love at the Last Resort* isn't happening. We gave up our charade."

I see Josh and Ollie exchange looks. Jac and Sylviane smirk at each other, and Johnny nudges Jac. Like they're all in on another big secret.

"What?" I stare down Jac.

Everyone takes a bite of a burger like they're on a synchronized eating team.

"You're like a lovesick puppy who's lost his way. Look at you, bro. You won't even talk about your oysters." Josh is the only one brave enough to volunteer anything.

"I'm not lovesick." I grab a handful of chips and stick them all into my mouth at once, making an obscene crunch.

They exchange looks again.

"What? What do you guys know?" Did Josh and Sylviane give the rest of them the scoop? The real intel?

"We know everything, mate." Johnny loves family drama.

Scratch that. Johnny loves any drama that has nothing to do with him.

"Everything, everything?" I ask.

"Yes. And we're sworn to secrecy. Our lips are sealed about the whole GG thing," Johnny offers, but I look at Jac.

"How do you feel about it? I mean, GG changed your life." If GG hadn't outed Johnny, they would have had more time together on the island. Fewer tears and sleepless nights for all of us.

"Yeah, but I know it wasn't Tippy then, and look how great everything is now."

She throws her arms around Johnny, who lavishes her with a huge kiss. Makes me want to throw up for real.

"Dave," says my dad. "We gather Tippy is GG." He looks around the table for confirmation. "And I think you underestimate the importance of GG on this island. You're just looking at it like it's a negative thing, but it's more than that. It connects each of us at a time when we can all be stuck on a screen. Have there been questionable comments? Of course. But aren't there with anything?"

"Tippy is more than a gossip column," adds Mom.

"I'm not sure she is." It's kind of her entire personality, and I'm mad at myself for not seeing it.

Mom starts in on me too. "She is, and GG is more than just gossip. It's the spirit of the island. GG's our cheerleader. And yes, sometimes our greatest critic. GG keeps us honest. She's an invisible string tying us all together. Don't dismiss Tippy because of this."

"She loves you," adds Sylviane.

"So I heard." Glad she blabbed it to everyone else too.

"Seems like you should give this thing a chance," says Ollie.

I was pretty clear about how I felt. And I'm pretty sure there's no room for discussion at this point.

"It's Dad's birthday, let's focus on that. Where are you guys going to travel first?"

"Oh, we have the best plan! Our first trip will be in June to Tofino!" Mom claps her hands.

"Where's that?" Johnny asks.

"Western side of Vancouver Island." Dad gets up and puts a few more burgers on the grill. "Supposed to have the best surfing in Canada."

"That will be great, since the two of you don't even surf," says Josh.

"It sure will be fun to see though. We're going to take a zodiac boat to the hot springs. Watch the bears. Go whale watching." Mom's practically giddy; she's like a teenager going on her first date. "I'm going to take my little cooking show on the road! Imagine how fun it will be in the RV! I can actually teach people something."

"Don't you want to give that thing up?" Hasn't she had enough embarrassment?

"Not really! It's fun!"

I should feel happier seeing Mom and Dad so excited about the next stage in their life, especially after dedicating so much time and money to us. They deserve this, but it makes me wonder if I'm ever going to get anything like that myself. For a hot second I thought there was hope, and then I remembered relationships are nothing but trouble.

I watch Jac and Johnny and Sylviane and Josh all throughout dinner and cake. While Sylviane and I are washing dishes, she looks at me and says, "You can get her back, you know."

My heart follows and we concoct a plan.

GREENSEA GAZETTE

Islanders,

Gossip forms bonds between people you don't know. It helps you give each other an extra smile in line at Island Grocers. A simple I-saw-that-too nod. Of course, some people don't like their name spilled in our little paper, but behave and you have nothing to worry about. It's rather simple. GG's mentions are never meant to harm. Rather just to share information.

So today, I'd like to reveal my identity. Not to put an end to the column, which turns out is a very necessary part of island life, but to end the secrecy and go back to the initial intent of the column: to share community information, not to Nancy Drew secrets out of islanders.

I, Tippy Meadowcroft, am GG. I took over approximately a year ago. I won't dishonor the previous GGs by sharing their identities. But I will let you know it's me, and I plan on continuing the column. I vow to do a better job and apologize for any times I've been mean spirited. I won't share your secrets UNLESS the greater community could benefit from them in any way. I'll continue to use my moniker, because honestly, I love it!

XOXO,

GG

TIPPY

I wake up certain Dave's going to pop up at Meadowcroft. And as the hours pass, I realize I'm wrong. Did he see my GG column? Did it make a difference? Maybe there's something more I can do. A bigger glow up to Sherman Shellfish. An article in a national news outlet. Dad has to have connections. My brain spins, and I start researching oyster farms. What have other people done? Dave's always going on about how those bivalves are saving the world. If there were more bivalves, it follows there'd be more saving. That's when the lightbulb goes on. What if we gave every Greensea resident on the water an oyster bag? What if everyone became an oyster farmer in their own right? Imagine how much good we could do then.

I sit and research some more. Since I can't exercise, I might as well work my mind. By the time I'm healed, Laura will have moved into my reformer. The pickleball court's gathering dust, and Bertha will need her chain greased and battery charged. The only thing I can do is walk. So I've walked mile after mile of Greensea's trails and worn a path on some back roads trying to burn some energy and calm my unhappy mind.

Sylviane wants me to go to the concert at Sunset Tower Park tonight. I told her I'd go if she walked a lap on the trail with me first and then promised to sit toward the back of the lawn near the tall fir trees so I wouldn't have to interact with too many people. I'm contemplating wearing a large hat and sunglasses. And maybe an oversized trench coat so no one recognizes me. But I have to rip the Band-Aid off sometime and face Greensea society.

She picks me up in Old Blue at four thirty sharp.

"What's up, buttercup?" she asks as I plop myself into the passenger seat, giving the car a once-over to make sure she doesn't have her pet rabbit with her. Her always-cheery personality is like nails on a chalkboard right now, but I bite my lip and mumble a, "Hi."

"Let's turn that frown upside down!"

I turn to stare her down. "I'm not in the mood for the Sunshine Sally act. I'm here because I'm feeling claustrophobic in my house."

"Got it." Sylviane pulls Old Blue out of the driveway and heads toward Sunset Tower Park.

"Not too cold today," Sylviane says and I nod. "Should have a decent sunset."

It's still early spring so it's prime golden hour, leaving the tower and the park glowing for the concert.

I decide to broach the topic of Dave. "So, I have a new idea that might win Dave back."

"Oh, really?" Her voice is an octave higher than usual. She lets out a nervous laugh. "This is about getting you out of the house. Let's not talk about anything stressful."

"Oookay." Message received. I won't talk about Dave.

She parks Old Blue, and I don't waste any time making a beeline for the walking path around the park. She knows better than to slow me down, so she just walks as fast as she can, breathing like she's summiting Mt. Rainier.

There's a steady stream of cars coming into the park, and the green's already dotted with picnic blankets and chairs. I forgot to look at the name of the band, but it really doesn't matter—Greensea will come out for any concert.

"Who's playing tonight?" I slow my pace a bit out of guilt.

"Oh! I think it's some brothers." She giggles. What's wrong with her? "I can't remember their name."

Probably the Banjo Brothers, a couple of Topper's friends who insert their lack of musical talent into every island event.

The sky's a perfect soft orange in between gray clouds I hadn't even noticed before. It's moments like these, the ones that you'd find on a postcard, that really reinforce the mistake the *Love at the Last Resort* people made. I'll boycott the show. Maybe GG will start a campaign encouraging islanders to join me.

We're approaching the trees, and Sylviane slows down.

"You can stay here. I've got a blanket in the car." She whips her phone out of her pocket and talks to someone as she walks over to the car.

The stage is all set. They've turned the lights on it, even though it's barely twilight. There's a keyboard, a couple of stools, and some microphones out. Bear and I came to two concerts last year with my Pilates peeps. Some bands made me wish I had headphones on, but a nice bottle of rosé can make everything better.

Sylviane walks back, spreads out an old plaid blanket, and puts a bag in the center.

"Some goodies for you." She takes out some cheese and crackers and hands me a mini can of wine.

"Thanks."

The banjo starts up, and the country twang of Dad's friends rings through the park. I gulp the wine to dull the sound. Sylviane's tapping her feet and clapping her hands like we're at a Johnny Nickel concert.

"Where's Josh, again?"

"He, umm, had something to do with his brothers. Helping their parents with the RV."

Something deep inside of me pangs. Dave's going about his business and not giving me a second thought. Figures. That's what I get for lying. I finally had a chance at love, even if it had been right in front of me my whole life, and I ruined it.

I notice a few people in front of us gawking at something. They're looking in our direction. Sylviane looks at me with a crooked smile.

"What?" I ask.

"Oh, nothing," she says, giggling. She's acting more unusual than normal.

"You're not telling me something. Is there something on my face? A hole in my pants?"

"Ugh! I can't do it anymore. I'm the worst at keeping secrets, which is weird because I'm a party magician and am supposed to have a good poker face!"

"Tell me now." My good arm's making a fist by my side. The other one's still in the sling.

"Look!" She points toward the water tower. I squint but can't really see anything against the orange sky. And then I see a figure, maybe two or three, on the tower.

"Who is that?" I'm scared to know the answer.

"Go look."

I speed walk toward the tower, Sylviane following behind. I squint a little more. Whoever's up there is graffitiing something.

TM + DS TL4E

I stop. Look at Sylviane. She nods her head, and I race to the bottom of the tower. Josh and Ollie are climbing down the single-file ladder on one of the legs. Dave's suspended in some rock climbing apparatus, putting the finishing touch on the *E*.

"Dave Sherman! What are you doing?"

He turns and looks down but ignores me and finishes his work.

Josh gets down and Sylviane hugs him.

"What's he thinking? That's illegal!" I hesitate and take a little step forward. "How's he going to get down?" I'm vacillating between the legality of the act, the fear he's going to get hurt, and fact of what those letters and that equation mean. Dave scooches toward the ladder and comes down.

After what feels like an eternity, he puts down his paintbrush and stands in front of me. "I wanted to make us permanent." He puts his hands on my hips.

People have gathered around us. I see a couple of phones taking pictures. Marlene from the Fit Greenies is giggling. Farrah yells, "Get it!" from a few yards away.

Dave reaches for the hand on my good arm. "All our teachers were right. It turns out I've been teasing you all these years because I liked attention from you...good or bad. Just took me a long time to realize it."

My heart slows to a more regular pace. Things might be okay.

"So you forgive me for lying to you?" I mean, his actions speak for themselves, but I need to hear him say the words too.

"It's come to my attention that you weren't really lying. You left out a few key details. More than forgiving, I'm accepting. You're right. We don't know everything about each other. But I'm ready to learn."

"Is this all a response to my column today?"

Dave looks at me with a furrowed brow. "No, haven't even read it. Why?"

I take my phone out of my pocket and pull the column up online. He takes a minute to read. "You outed yourself."

"Yep. No reason the column needs to be anonymous. If everyone knows it's me, it'll keep me honest."

"Did you feel forced to do that?" Dave hangs his head down.

"No. I think it's for the best. Dad and I talked about it, and all the positive parts of GG are still intact even if people know who's writing it."

I sat with Dad for hours last night, trying to come up with the right strategy. The truth is, I like being GG, and I don't want to give it up. I held hope in the back of my mind that Dave would read the column and find his way back to me. It's kind of more than I could have imagined that he was simultaneously working on a plan.

I look up at him. "You thought the best way to get me back was breaking the law at the park?"

"Well, I thought it was a good way to get your attention. And the only way I knew how to make this all permanent."

Dave puts his arm around me and I lean my head against him. "Are we good?" His whisper sends chills down my back.

I look at him and whisper, "TL4E…"

His hand reaches behind my back and pulls me toward him. His lips find mine and I wish I could teleport us back to Meadowcroft. Instead, the crowd cheers and I swear I hear Mayor Nickerbottom saying he knew from the get-go this was true love.

We pull apart and I look at him. He's got some paint in his hair, not from me this time. I reach up to touch it and then he takes my hand in his. We raise our arms like we've just won an epic pickleball match. The Banjo Brothers play and the crowd cheers even more. Golden hour has a whole new meaning.

We're ready to write the rest of our ferry tale. Greensea-style.

GREENSEA GAZETTE

Dear Islanders,

Dave Sherman pulled out all the stops, making sure everyone on the island knows he and Tippy (should I refer to myself in the first person now that I've done the grand reveal? Or do you still want to pretend I'm an anonymous being? I'm sure you have opinions.) are for real now. For all those wondering, Dave used permanent paint as evidenced by his new red bangs. Best of luck, Dave, she's a lot. Insert winky face. As far as ferry tales go, was this one more "Frog Prince" or "Rapunzel?" I'm sure the MCs have their own opinion, and we'll let the readers decide for themselves.

The Frickenshaws of Grays Bay have added an interesting element to their property: three swan boats. The kind you pedal from place to place. Are they hoping to take over the ferry ballet show? Could these sweet little boats be used as water taxis? This author is jealous that she didn't think of this ingenious idea.

Swan boats moving from place to place in the harbor? Next level! That's some top-tier thinking, Frickenshaws!

XOXO,

GG

AFTERWORD

TIPPY

A Hollywood TV set has nothing on Greensea! Johnny left me in charge of turning downtown into a festive little area for his big proposal. I had dozens and dozens of twinkling fairy lights strung from the town gazebo to The Old Owl. Mrs. Harris' class cut and hung paper snowflakes from every tree down Main Street. Hanging baskets filled with winter-white flowers and evergreens hang from all the summer spots. I even decked some of the lampposts out in garland, because why not! It's like a Hallmark movie threw up on Greensea.

The music teacher at the elementary school taught the kids how to play "Greensea Gal," so there's a full band waiting for Johnny and Jac's arrival at the gazebo. Saltwater Bakeshop baked cookies in the shape of Hello Kitty keys to commemorate their first meeting, when Jac tried to stab Johnny with a key. And I had *Team Jac and Johnny* signs made up too. It's quaint and true island style in a flash mob kind of way.

And of course, the rest of the town is holiday ready with the tree in the center of the village green. The hardware store donned dozens of screwdrivers hung in the shape of a Christmas tree. Island Grocers has a magical woodland scene complete with papier mâché mushrooms and gnomes. And The Corner Joint has a snowman made of CBD gummies in the front window.

Johnny paced around Meadowcroft this morning, going over all the last details, while Jac flew up from San Francisco without suspecting a thing.

"Tippy!" Johnny whisper-shouts to me in the ferry terminal parking lot.

"You can talk normally! She's in the middle of the Sound and can't hear you!"

"What's that smell?"

I look around me and sniff. No weird Greensea animals or people leaving us a present. I sniff again. It's fresh and crisp. A little wet. Filled with fir. Snow! "I smell snow!"

He grabs both of my hands and looks in my eyes. "I love snow!" He sticks his tongue out and catches one of the three flakes falling from the sky.

It's beautiful and magical, but we need to get in our spots.

Johnny has Mr. Jackson and his horse and buggy ready to pick Jac up when she gets off the ferry. I shoo him off into the carriage. I'm hiding in the bushes with a clear view of the carriage and the ferry terminal. I've got binoculars around my neck and a walkie talkie ready to give Dave, who's hiding at the village green, a signal when the happy couple leaves the area. It's so romantic I can hardly stand it!

Jac walks off the ferry and looks around, not expecting to be picked up in a horse and buggy, but I see Johnny jump out of the back, and I hear her squeal.

"Ten-four, Oyster Man. The subjects are on their way."

"Ten-four, Gossip Girl." Dave and I had fun making up codenames.

I get on Bertha and take the trail to the village green. Dave's got himself tucked in a cove of pine trees.

I love a production. This may not be the scale I had in mind with *Love at the Last Resort*, but it will still go down in history books and maybe even get a mention in *People* magazine.

The clippity clop of the horse's hooves gets closer.

"This is so exciting." I reach over to Dave and give him a peck on his cheek. He grabs my hips and pulls me in for a proper kiss, accidentally pushing my walkie talkie button...and some other buttons I'd rather think about in the privacy of one of our own homes. I give him a little push away.

"Not now!" I can't help but laugh, because a few months ago I never thought we'd be at this place.

I see swans near the gazebo and they're getting pretty close to the horse, causing it to neigh. I grab my walkie talkie. "Mystery Girl! Why are the swans out?" It's out of character for Sylviane to mess something up.

"Because I thought you gave me the signal."

Shit. Dave pulled me in and the walkie-talkie went off early. "Get them back!"

I see Sylviane and Josh run toward the swans, shooing them back into the makeshift pen with no luck. Mr. Jackson pulls back on the reins, but the horse gallops. I watch Johnny put his arm across Jac, and I hear Johnny yell as they gallop past the gazebo, past The Old Owl, and down to Grays Bay.

Just as they're about to go into the water, I hear more yelling.

"Hold on!" yells Mr. Jackson again. "Whoa, Chestnut! HALT! I said WHOA!"

Chestnut doesn't care, and Mr. Jackson yells it again.

The buggy lurches forward, and Chestnut comes to an abrupt stop in the sand. Johnny and Jac go forward, but his arms stop her before she hits the front of the carriage.

Shit. Shit. Shit. This was not how the plan was supposed to go! Almost killing Johnny and Jac was not on my itinerary. There's a mob of excited islanders moving toward them. Dave and I run over to Sylviane and Josh.

"What the hell?" I ask, but there's really no time for explanations. We watch as Johnny hops out of the carriage and drops to one knee.

"Jac, this is not at all how I expected this to go. Not one moment of it. But I guess things have been like that for us since the beginning, and I'm not sure why I thought this would have been any different. I love you. I love the way you tried to stab me with a house key. I love the way you didn't blink when I picked you up in a horse and buggy. I love that you call me out on all of my shit and keep me grounded."

The whole town is moving closer now, and Johnny's speech is picking up its pace.

"I love that every day is a surprise with you." He looks at the crowd and speaks even faster. "Jac Sherman, will you do me the honor of marrying me?"

"Wait! Wait! Wait," yells someone who sounds like Mayor Nickerbottom. "The band is coooooommming!"

But Johnny opens a box and Jac drops and kneels next to him. He takes the ring out of the box and puts it on her finger.

"Is that a yes?" he asks. She can only nod her head. They laugh and tumble over in the sand just as a trombone starts up, followed quickly by a squeaky clarinet, in their rendition of "Greensea Gal."

Dave wraps me up and lifts me. "Nice job, girlfriend."

I shrug. "All's well that ends well, I guess."

I've planned a family party, with the help of Bell, to celebrate at The Old Owl. No animals or townspeople for this part of the night. Just the Sherman Family, significant others, and Jac's best friend, Daisy. Bell and I transformed the place. More fairy lights everywhere, because twinkly lights make everything look fantastic. The tables are covered in green Indian block tablecloths. We made the centerpieces out of greens and disco balls. The fairy lights dance off the disco balls, and the whole place looks magical.

Johnny and Jac come in. She squeals when she sees Daisy. "What? How did you get here?"

Daisy hugs her and grabs her finger to look at the ginormous ring. "Johnny flew me in, and Oliver picked me up at the airport yesterday. I can't believe my best friend's getting married! Again!" They squeal some more and hug.

Dave walks over and gives me a hug. "This is amazing. Those producers sure missed out on quite an opportunity to work with you."

"About that…"

I'm interrupted by a bubbly Jac running over with Johnny. She wraps me in an enormous hug.

"Johnny told me you're responsible for all of this! Thank you!"

"Well, yes. And sorry about the swans!"

"No worries, mate! No one can control wild animals! Not even the great Tippy!"

Johnny's right. I can't blame myself.

"Tippy, Dave, will you both be in our wedding?" Jac is practically radiating glitter, she's so happy.

I look at Dave and he looks at me, and we say, "Of course!" in unison.

Dave wraps his arms around me. "What was it you were going to tell me before?"

"Oh, nothing. Tonight's not the time to discuss all my other diabolical plans." I giggle and bring my lips to his.

GREENSEA GAZETTE

Dear Islanders,

Unless you've been living under Greensea Goat, you've heard about the engagement of Johnny and Jac. There is no doubt that event will live in the Annals of Greensea History for quite a bit of time. We hear all the Sherman brothers and their significant others (me!) will be in the wedding party! Bound to be quite an affair!

Mayor Nickerbottom would like to convene a town meeting to discuss the upcoming nuptials. Buckle your seatbelts, the Royal Greensea Wedding is sure to be something none of us will ever forget!

XOXO,

GG

THANKS FOR READING!

Let's keep in touch...

ACKNOWLEDGMENTS

Thank you for loving Greensea! It means so much to me! I couldn't have done any of this without an amazing team by my side. As I sit here, trying to write a proper thank you to everyone, I realize I'm surrounded by some truly incredible humans. Over the last year, I've met more writers in my community and deepened bonds with those I already knew. Guys, I'm so lucky! I love being a part of BARN, meeting new people, and learning new skills. Put yourself out there—it's worth it every time!

The local businesses have been beyond generous with their support of my books, and I'm so grateful to live in a community like this.

Thank you, Amberly at Watermark Writing Company, for all your editing and support.

Thank you to my Pilates instructor for inspiring me, centering me, and strengthening both my core and my soul. Thanks to all the women I've bonded with as we work out on that ancient torture device.

To my fellow PTSO peeps—yes, I made fun of us, but you know how much I love and appreciate you! I joke about volunteering, but it's been such a big and important part of my life for the last few decades. I have no idea what I'll do once the twins graduate. Support your local school volunteers—they do important, often invisible work.

I'm so lucky to have a team of early readers—you know who you are, and I adore you. My mom and Gill have been reading and cheering me on from afar all these years, and a book isn't ready until you've both read it!

Jen—business partner, cover designer, editor, proofreader, fellow Lynn, and most importantly, dear friend—this venture is nothing without you. I'm looking forward to what's ahead.

To my favorite beeyatches—this is a contest. The first one to make it to the acknowledgments gets a prize! You're all the best cheerleaders. Thank you, Justin, for creating a world that allows me to follow my dreams. Kids, thanks for letting me mash up our life and add it to my fiction. You're my everything. Safety Mom loves you.

ABOUT THE AUTHOR

Julie Farley loves writing books filled with big families, lots of heart, and plenty of laughs. She lives on an island in the Pacific Northwest with her husband and four amazing kids. Julie has a bachelor's degree from the University of Notre Dame and a graduate degree from DePaul University. When she's not busy with her family or writing books, you'll find her watching reality TV...of any sort!

ABOUT THE PUBLISHER

Fog House Press is an independent boutique publishing company offering authors a comprehensive suite of services to ensure their work shines. Our mission is to empower authors to tell their best story by providing full professional publishing services, as well as a host of individual offerings.

ALSO BY JULIE FARLEY

Love Songs and Ferry Tales
Cozy Cabins and Ferry Tales

Tripped Up Love
The New Ever After
Another Tomorrow

www.ingramcontent.com/pod-product-compliance
Lightning Source LLC
Chambersburg PA
CBHW022124310726
48972CB00007B/2184